DISASTER CREEK

DISASTER CREEK

D. B. Newton

GUNSMOKE

First published in the UK by Hale

This hardback edition 2009
by BBC Audiobooks Ltd
by arrangement with
Golden West Literary Agency

ISBN 978 1 405 68263 3

British Library Cataloguing in Publication Data available.

Printed and bound in Great Britain by
CPI Antony Rowe, Chippenham and Eastbourne

DISASTER CREEK

Chapter 1

Ed Bannon saw the dust rising above a belt of timber ahead and to the left of him, perhaps a mile off the stage road he'd been following west from Canyon City. A low afternoon sun turned the dust into a plume, golden against the deep Oregon sky. From curiosity he pulled the dun horse in for a moment to look at it.

At first glance he had taken the dust plume for a sign of cattle being driven, or maybe antelope or wild mustangs moving through the dry hills. But minutes passed and nothing broke out of the trees, while the yellow stain continued to hang motionless save for a slight raveling and drift before the constant push of hot west wind. Whatever caused the dust seemed to be holding stationary. Thinking it over, Bannon took off his hat, ran the fingers of one hand through thick-growing black hair, and then sat holding the hat while he listened to the immense stillness and let that wind on his forehead dry the scalding moisture that had collected below the sweatband.

Man and horse and gear alike were without flash and serviceable. So was the wooden-handled Colt he sometimes carried in his saddle roll but which was belted around his waist now, in a scarred leather holster, where he could get at it. He was a young man still, only a trifle over average height but compactly built. His glance was direct and restless, seldom still, missing nothing. Like the mouth, bracketed by deep lines beneath a full black moustache, his eyes seemed to have forgotten something of the knack of smiling.

By the time he pulled the hat on again and adjusted the chin strap, he had made up his mind. Riding blind, in unfamiliar country, he would have felt uneasy to go any farther without making sure of that dust. On this decision he pulled off of the stage road and instead sent the dun horse down the slope that fell away southward, toward that motionless banner of yellow with the blue Ochoco ridges piling up on the horizon behind it.

Except for the sheer immensity of it, he hadn't found this a particularly beautiful country—lava-rimmed, thin-soiled, and eroded, with scant timber to break the endless sweep of bunchgrass bending under the constant wind. The empty swells of grass held a crisscross of stock trails and Bannon picked one of these and followed it down into the belt of timber and through it. Almost sooner than he expected, he found what he was looking for.

It was a mustanger's outfit. There was the crudest kind of dugout, hacked into the dry flank of a hill and finished off with slabs of rock and lengths of juniper pole; it had a brush roof and a single window and door. A spring had been rocked up to make a pool, and an open-fronted shed served for storage. More important to the layout was the battery of corrals, three good-sized ones, sturdily built of juniper poles. A pair of horses stood hipshot in one of them; in another a half dozen or so milled restlessly. The third structure was the breaking pen, and he could see this was the source of the dust that had drawn him here. As Bannon approached, a sturdy-looking black was being put through its paces, its sides glistening with sweat and streaked with the lava dust that rose about horse and rider in a yellow cloud. Bannon drew rein to watch the battle.

He had seen fancier rides at rodeos, but this was being done for business, not for show. It was a silent contest, except for the rhythmic jar of hooves pounding the earth and the grunting of breath expelled from the black's lungs. The rider, a slat-lean fellow in worn denims, wasn't the least interested in style; he was methodically riding the black horse down, and he had one hand clamped firmly on the saddle horn to help hold him there. He had lost his hat, and wings of unshorn, graying hair seemed about to be torn leaping from his head with every drive of the animal's four braced legs.

But the stud was tiring fast. He was laboring now; pure effort showed in the way he gathered his strength for each crowhopping lunge, and to Bannon it was plainly just a matter of time. Even as he watched, the stud tried a few last halfhearted lunges and then suddenly stumbled and nearly went to his knees. He caught himself and tried no more, but came to a stand on widespread legs, beaten, head sagging and sweat dripping into the dust as his sides worked like bellows to fill tortured lungs.

There was no show of triumph from the rider. For long moments, as the curtains of dust shook out and began to settle, he remained with his head on his chest and looking almost as badly used as the black stud. Slowly, then, he pulled his leg across and stepped down. When his boots touched earth he simply broke; his legs buckled under him and he went down in a sprawl on his face.

Bannon was already coming out of the saddle. When he slid between the rails, the black shied away on dragging hoofs into a far corner, and he gave the animal no attention. Bending over the rider, Bannon now saw a spot of blood on the right leg of the man's faded jeans. Bannon pulled the jeans leg up and found a red-soaked bandage partially covered by the high top of the man's scuffed boot.

The horsebreaker was stirring and beginning to swear, feebly but luridly. Ed Bannon said gruffly, "Let's get you out of here." The man was all bone and hard muscle, not heavy but awkward to manage since he did little to help himself. Somehow Bannon got him through the bars and eased him to the ground a little distance from the corral, with his back against a juniper stump. The man, who looked to be on the upward side of forty, scowled up at the stranger through dust and sweat coating a lantern-jawed face that was burned brick red by years of sun and wind. He demanded gruffly, "Who the hell are you?"

Ed Bannon ignored the question. "Mister," he said, "don't you know you've got a boot full of blood?"

The other man grunted, irritable with pain. "Would you believe I shot myself in the leg? Yesterday morning, it was—dropped my gun and the damn thing went off . . ." He made a move to rise, thought better of it, and sank back, swearing. But he had rallied enough now, and he set about trying to remove the boot. Bannon saw he wasn't going to get the job done and leaned to help. Between them they worked it off, at the expense of a grunt of pain from the hurt mustanger.

The blood-soaked wrapping came away, revealing a shallow bullet groove sliced along the outer muscle of the calf. "Looks painful," Bannon commented.

"Stings a mite," the other conceded tightly. He added, "There's water inside there on the table, and some clean rags. I'd be much obliged." Bannon nodded and went to fetch them.

The dugout was no more than he would have expected—cramped quarters even for a man living alone. The mustanger had a bunk against one wall, a table and a couple of stools made of slab, a packing case converted to shelves for storing odds and ends of supplies. For cooking there was a hearth that was little more than a fire pit, with an escape hole above it to carry smoke away on the draft. A plank door and window shutter leaned handy, to be put up in bad weather.

A tin basin and a bucket of spring water were on the table, and Bannon found the rags that had been torn up from old flour sacking. He filled the basin and seeing a half-empty whiskey bottle took that along as he returned to the hurt man. The latter grabbed the bottle, drained off a good part of what was left in it. Then, ramming the cork home with the heel of a palm, he dipped a rag in the water and began to soak the dirt and blood from his wound.

Bannon remarked, "You say you did that yesterday? It's never going to heal if you don't stay off the leg and give it a chance."

"Man has to make a living," the other grunted. "I got a half dozen head under contract for gentling and delivery. Don't look like I'm gonna get the job done."

Bannon looked toward the breaking pen where the black stud appeared to have recovered his wind and was moving around a little; he seemed bothered by the saddle on his back. "It was a pretty fair ride you gave him, all the same—whatever it may have done to *you*."

"It's the third time I topped him—and I ain't done more'n knock off a few of the rough corners. Lot of these range scrubs don't have any real fight in 'em. Once in a while, though, you bring in a salty one like the black, and he can have the makings of a pretty fair horse if he's broke right. But looks like I've gone as far with him as I'm going!" He added, "If you would, you might take the gear off and throw the sonofabitch in with the rest. I'm through with him."

"All right." Bannon returned to the breaking pen. The black—still very much a wild horse—rolled his eyes and pawed the dust uneasily at the hated sight and human scent of him, but he calmed and stood trembling as soon as Bannon caught hold of the bridle. The saddle and blanket came off and were hung on the top fence pole; then Bannon led him through the gate into the larger holding corral to join the others. While he was about it, he grabbed up a handful of hay and used this to rub the black down, getting rid of some of the sweat and mud that streaked his barrel and legs; though he trembled, the horse stood still for it. Afterward Bannon removed the bridle and turned the stud loose and went through the bars to rejoin the mustanger.

The latter was rebandaging his wounded leg. Bannon tossed down the bridle and stood watching him a moment. He said, "I suppose you know this country pretty well?"

"As well as most," the older man told him. "Been trappin' horses over a lot of it, ten years and more—selling 'em across the state, clear down into Nevada."

"Then you can probably tell me: if I was wanting to head south, is there a good route from here?"

"You mean straight into the Ochocos?" The mustanger indicated the country roughing up toward the barrier of piney hills. He shook his head emphatically. "No, sir! Wouldn't advise anyone bucking those hills who didn't know 'em. You want to make any time, you keep to the roads. You got a choice of two routes. The best one's to go east to Canyon City and then south of there, pick up the Silvies and foller that river down to the Malheur country. Or you can head west through the mountains on the wagon road to Prineville—once you climb out of that Crooked River gorge, you can find your own way south."

Bannon, who had already been through Canyon City, wanted to know how far it was to Prineville. The man thumbed his lantern jaw as he thought. "Sixty-odd miles, anyway. Couple of good days' ride."

"I guess that answers my question." And then, as casually as he could make it sound, Bannon added, "Oh—you wouldn't by any chance have seen another rider passing through? Tall fellow, sandy-headed, probably clean-shaven. Has an old scar here." He touched a thumb to his right cheek.

The mustanger had been draining off the last of the whiskey. Now he lowered his emptied bottle as he peered at the stranger. "No, can't say I've run into anybody like that." A slyness came into the narrow, wind-whipped face. "Would you be looking for him? Or—is he looking for *you?*" He couldn't have missed the sudden stiffening of the other man; he didn't wait to get an answer. Abruptly he flung the bottle aside, to smear an arc of reflected light from the setting sun and shatter against a rock. He picked up his boot and hoisted himself to his feet. When he put his weight on the injured leg, he staggered painfully and windmilled one gaunt arm to keep from falling.

Stiffly, his manner cold in the wake of the other's probing, Ed Bannon said, "Looks like you can manage—though if you expect that leg to get well, you better stay off it till it does," He added, "I guess I'll be riding." And he turned toward the ground-anchored dun.

He was reaching for the reins when the mustanger said, "You don't have to rush off. Looks to me you been pushing that horse pretty hard, and there's nothing at all betwixt here and the next town—Mitchell, that is, a good dozen miles farther. Be sunset before long. I got some fair venison stew to warm up, and you're more'n welcome to spend the night." He added, as though it were an afterthought, "I just might have a proposition to offer you."

Bannon hesitated. He was frankly dubious about any proposition that might come from this source, but the mention of stew interested him; his saddle pockets were empty except for some cold biscuits and jerky, though of course the other man had no way of knowing that. He nodded finally. "All right." And because it was only polite, after you'd accepted an invitation to break bread with someone, he added, "The name's Ed Bannon."

The mustanger acknowledged it with an incurious nod. "Cap Flynn . . ."

It was all as informal as that.

The smallest of the three corrals contained a couple of horses that, from their saddle marks, Bannon judged to be the mustanger's work string. He unsaddled the dun and put it in with them, and afterward took it on himself to see that all the stock had feed from a stack of cut hay he found under the brush-roof shelter. He decided that would be a good place to spread his blankets, since it appeared he would be spending the night and there didn't look to be room for him in the dugout.

By the time he finished his chores, the sun had dropped from sight and the sky was already deepening toward first dark. It promised another fine night ahead, without clouds, though the steady wind would turn chilly as the earth gave back the heat it had stored during the day. He had heard that even a July night could bring frost, on occasion, to this high plateau country of central Oregon. When he entered the dugout, ducking its low doorway, Cap Flynn was hobbling around, dishing up the stew into tin plates from the pan where he'd been heating it in the coals of the fire pit; they ate by the light of a candle stuck by its own grease in a niche in the rock wall. The mustanger had turned talkative, and he regaled his guest with stories of his experiences in tracking down and trapping wild range stock.

Bannon gathered that it was a hard life and a minimal existence, eased on occasion when Cap Flynn managed to trap an animal worth selling to the U. S. Cavalry or to a rancher at something better than the going price for the usual sort of wild scrub. In the long run, working alone as he had to, he probably got little enough reward for his long hours and backbreaking, chancy labor, aside from indulging a fierce independence.

Flynn seemed completely incurious about his

guest or his background or his intentions. But then, out of a moment's silence, he suddenly came up with a suggestion; and Bannon recognized that this, at last, was the proposition he had mentioned: "You like to make twenty bucks?"

Ed Bannon took his time answering with a noncommittal question. "Doing what?"

"Nothing much, really. If you're heading for Prineville, it won't even be off your road. I mentioned earlier I had some stock under contract—a half dozen head—for the livery stable over in Mitchell. The old man there takes quite a few of these broncs off my hands. Uses some for rent animals, sells some to the ranchers or to people travelin' through on the stage road. It all helps."

"And you want me to deliver these horses?" Bannon formed a triangle with his elbows on the table, and the tin coffee cup held steaming before his face. Over the brim of the cup he looked narrowly at the other man.

"Why not? You'll be going right through there tomorrow."

"A half dozen head of horses—even range scrubs—are worth something," Bannon pointed out. "Especially if the black is one of them. I'm a stranger. How do you know you can trust them to me?"

Cap Flynn lifted narrow shoulders in a shrug. "Call it a hunch. I do know I ain't in shape to make the ride myself right now—not ride and handle a string of mustangs same time I'm trying to look after this bum leg. Like you say, I got to lay off it and give the damn thing a chance to heal.

"You get to Mitchell, just tell old man Tracy I said to give you the twenty in cash and put the balance to my credit. Or maybe I better write him a note and explain why I never finished this batch off before turning them over to him, like I usually do." The mustanger stirred sugar into his ink-black coffee. "Of course," he went on mildly, when Bannon didn't immediately answer, "if you don't want to do this for me, guess I can wait and see if maybe that other feller drifts by—the one you mentioned, sandy-haired and with a scar on his cheek? He might could be more obliging . . ."

For just a moment, then, his glance locked with the stranger's and there was the least hint of a threat that worked its way into the stillness of the dugout. The choice Cap Flynn offered was clear enough: It was a crude kind of blackmail. Bannon let his resentment show in the cold look he gave the man through the curtain of steam rising between his hands.

But after that, he eased the stiffness from his shoulders and made his eyes expressionless as he drained off the strong contents of the cup. "Well," he said briefly, setting it down, "I guess any man can use twenty dollars."

Thus it was settled, and at once Cap Flynn showed all his teeth in a grin that struck across his red-burned features. "I do take this most kindly," he assured his guest. "Find yourself a place to spread your blankets and we'll send you off in good time, come morning." The grin never altered as he added, looking directly into the other man's face, "And if any stranger of any kind should come asking questions—why, I never seen you. Hell, I never seen nobody at all!"

Chapter 2

It had to be something in the morning itself that fretted her, Kit Tracy thought—a hint of wildness carried on the wind that breathed through the shallow canyon at her feet, where much of the town lay huddled; there was a scent of the land itself, of the dark dampness of Bridge Creek below her, of pine smoke from breakfast fires, of fruit ripening on the trees of Sasser's orchard and in the lush gardens of nearly every village residence. It all somehow combined to work at her in troubling ways. It held her motionless here at the edge of the bluff in her best white Sunday dress, with the flounces at the shoulders and the belted waist and full, ankle-length skirt, her Bible clutched forgotten in one gloved hand.

Behind her, the bell in the church steeple sent its summoning strokes all along the stillness of Piety Hill, and now she heard someone impatiently calling her name. That was her best friend, Addie Weiker, waiting on the church steps and no doubt wondering what ever could have got into her. Kit turned and waggled her fingers in answer, but for some reason she felt unable to move from where she stood.

She could hardly explain herself. At twenty, Kit Tracy was not a willful or disobedient girl, and in a village as small as Mitchell, Oregon, there were so few distractions that she usually looked forward to Sunday church service. But this particular summer morning, with the bright sun and a sky filled with great floating castles of cloud, she somehow didn't seem able to close herself even for an hour into the confinement of walls and the drone of a dull sermon—not when the winy air appeared on the verge of saying something, if she could only understand what it was trying to tell her.

The voice of the bell was suspended, leaving a pulsing stillness. Addie called again, a note of alarm creeping in: "Kit, what *is* the matter with you? Do you want to be late? They're about to start without you! Now, come *on!*" Kit only nodded without looking around, aware of the enormity of this but refusing to obey. All her neighbors and friends would be settling themselves in the pews; her grandmother would be keeping her usual place for her, at a loss to know what could have happened. Even as she hesitated, Kit heard the first strains of the pump organ setting the key for the opening hymn.

But at the same time she became aware of another sound growing in the morning, one she had not expected; it made her peer again up the canyon. To her right, from beyond Max Putz's flour mill and the bend in the creek that screened the canyon's southern end from view, a spatter of hoof sound swelled and echoed off the sounding boards of rocky hillsides. Something seemed to turn over inside her, almost as though this was an answer to her strange mood of anticipation. Just how many horses were coming down the creek trail, it would be hard to judge. They seemed to be moving at no great speed, maybe a comfortable walk. And now the first one came into sight, a dun with a rider up. A towrope trailed from his saddle horn. And after him came the others—a half dozen, tied head to tail and strung out behind the rider.

The angle was bad and the distance too great to tell her much, but she could see the way they moved. They looked like range horses, only recently caught—mustangs like the ones her grandfather occasionally dealt in. Most would be little more than scrubs; but one big fellow immediately held her attention. He headed the string, a black with a coat that looked good even from here, and he showed signs of real spirit. When the buildings of town began to close around him he plainly didn't like them; he started balking and fighting the towrope, threatening to rouse the scruffy-looking claybank behind him and spread a contagion back down the line. The rider had to turn and try to settle him; the black shook out his mane and his hooves danced around a little and an angry trumpeting broke from him on the morning stillness.

Kit felt the breath catch in her throat as she heard the black. He might be only a scrub, but she was someone who loved horses, both from instinct and from training, and the savage protest had something that spoke to her own strange mood.

With the next breath she was thinking, *Why, these must be Grandpa's horses!* They could hardly be meant for anyone else, and with Orin Tracy away at the county seat, there was no one but a simple-minded hostler on hand to receive them. She owed it to Grandpa to fill in for him. . . . It was all the excuse she needed, one anybody would have to accept. Pausing for no more than a final wave and a shake of the head at Addie Weiker, she stooped swiftly to catch up the hem of her skirt. She could picture her friend's scandalized expression as Addie watched her disappear down the steep wooden stairs to the bottom of the canyon.

To Kit, who had lived here nearly all her twenty years, it seemed perfectly natural to build a town on two levels—the houses, where most people lived, up on the bench a hundred feet higher than the business section on the canyon floor beside the creek. She felt at home here, in upper and lower town alike. She knew every foot of it—except of course for the interiors of the saloons, which she glimpsed only through their swinging half doors as she hurried past. Now she took the steps with Bible and skirt in one gloved hand, the other trailing the uneven handrail; and she never stopped to think that her best Sunday dress might be out of place, down on the shaly flat by the creek where men were already collecting to see the arrival of a half dozen wild horses on a rope.

This was horse country, and though the denizens of the lower town might not share an enthusiasm for attending church service, there was hardly anyone who failed to respond to the sight of anything on hooves—even mustangs such as these. As she came nearer she could see that their interest was centered on the black stud that had caught her eye. Seen at this level he looked bigger, and under the dust there was a good sheen to his coat. He drew back on the rope that held him anchored, a proud arch to his neck as he rolled his eyes and snorted at the hostile smells of the men crowding around him. Most of the comments Kit overheard, punctuated with profanity, were in admiring tribute to the black.

At first, as she halted at a discreet distance to observe what was going on, she could see nothing of the rider; he had left his animals standing in the street, the reins of the dun saddle horse tossed in a rough tie over a hitching post to hold it. But now she caught sight of him. He was up on the porch of a store, trying the door and seemingly surprised to find it locked—perhaps he had forgotten it was Sunday, when most places of business would be closed. He turned away and the hat brim hid his eyes as he looked over the crowd taking shape around the horses. "Better back away," he told them shortly. "You're making them nervous."

He came down the plank steps to join the men, and Kit got an impression he was asking questions, seeking information he hadn't been able to get at the store that was locked. She heard her grandfather's name, saw someone point out the livery barn and corral farther along the canyon. Nodding his thanks, the stranger turned back to the horses; he seemed not to have noticed a quartet of latecomers who sauntered over now from a deadfall across the street, elbowing a way for themselves through the fringe of onlookers.

Kit Tracy saw, and had a feeling they might be about to give the stranger a hard moment or two—it all depended on the unpredictable moods of their leader. Reub Springer, she could have told him, had a bad reputation.

All four moved directly in on the half-wild horses, causing an uneasy stirring along the towrope. The stranger turned quickly at that, and the good humor left his voice as he said sharply, "I said leave them alone!"

Springer ignored the warning. He might have been thought too slow-witted to know he had been warned, but more likely he felt too arrogantly sure of himself to care—Reub Springer wasn't stupid, or he wouldn't have held the important job he did with John Luft's ranch crew. He was tough, a big man, and solid. He had a chest like a barrel and shoulders that made his head look small, though it was heavily boned across the forehead and the jaw. Most people she knew were cautiously respectful, if not outright afraid of him. Kit Tracy was almost certain he had killed at least one man, either with those big fists of his or with the gun he liked to wear openly on one slabby thigh.

He punched the sweat-marked hat back from his face and, looking critically along the string of animals, said with an open sneer, "Bunch of scrubs, I'd call 'em. Hell, you couldn't give them to me!"

The stranger retorted, "I wasn't figuring to."

One of Springer's companions suggested, "What about the black, though? Reub, I think you'd have to say that's some horse." And he put out a hand as though to take the halter and pull the animal's head around for a better look. The stud reacted at once, with a walling of his eyes and a quick twist and reach of bared teeth. The cowboy swore and jerked his hand away.

"You were told about that!" the stranger snapped.

The cowboy looked a little shaken. He rubbed the hand across his shirt. "Mean sonofabitch, ain't he?"

Reub Springer snickered briefly. "Me, I kind of like that," he said. "In a horse *or* a man . . ."

And Kit Tracy thought with disdain: *You would!* Reub Springer was mean himself. You could see it in his face—in the nose that lay flat from being broken in some past brawl, the little eyes that peered from beneath bristling brows, the scarred cheeks glinting faintly red with beard stubble.

Not getting any answer to his comment, the big man pressed for one. "Mister, did you hear what I said?"

That got him a look, as though in mild surprise. "Why, no. Was I supposed to be listening?"

"I was saying, a man or a horse that won't put up a fight ain't worth bothering with."

The stranger considered that a moment in silence; it seemed to Kit he must surely recognize he was being baited. If so, he refused to give any sign. He turned away and lifted a saddle fender to check the cinch on the dun. Reub Springer appeared baffled for the moment—Kit could almost read the emotions that crossed his battered face. Then he must have decided on his next move; he settled his shoulders and said, in a new tone, "The longer I look at the black, the more he reminds me of a bronc I had in my string six months back. He jumped a corral fence and got away from me and I ain't seen him since. But right now"—he went on pitching his voice louder—"I'm saying this is the same horse. You hear? I'm saying he belongs to me—and what's your answer to that?"

This time the stranger straightened up and looked directly at the big man, as though finally aware that he was going to have to be dealt with. He took his deliberate time. He said, "I take it your name isn't Orin Tracy . . ."

A sneer split the man's mouth. "Do I look like I was eighty years old?"

"No. And the way you use your mouth, I'd say it's doubtful you'll ever make it! As for the horses, they belong to this man Tracy, and I've been hired to deliver them. It doesn't leave you and me anything more to talk about." Without haste he turned his back on the big man, hooked the saddle horn with the fist that held the reins, and swung lightly astride. Reub Springer had a look of bafflement on him as the stranger kicked his mount with a blunt spur. The dun led off at a walk, the string of horses holding back an instant before falling into motion. And the knot of men stood silent to watch them go.

As he drew even with Kit, she had her first real look at the stranger's darkly weathered face, with its black moustache and restless eyes. The eyes cut to her, drawn by the hand she lifted—she had been about to call out and let him know she was the granddaughter of the man he sought here at Mitchell. But as she opened her mouth she caught a glimpse of movement and what came from her instead was a warning: *"Watch out!"*

The stranger didn't hesitate. A jerk of his left hand on the reins brought the dun about in a turn, swinging him clear of the horses, and she saw then that he had a gun and had been holding it unobtrusively against his right leg—a precaution that showed this man was not going to be caught foolishly off guard. He had evidently spotted the thing that startled Kit: big Reub Springer standing, spread-legged, with a gun half drawn. Now, seeing a weapon already pointed at him, Springer halted the move as if his arm had frozen; his face contorted in surprise and anger, and behind him the onlookers scattered like quail.

Not a word was said, but the gun leveled in the stranger's hand conveyed its own message. In dead silence Reub Springer stared at it, and his face slowly turned a darker red and the thick chest within his red-and-black checked shirt seemed to swell. It appeared to cost him an effort when he opened his fingers and let the half-drawn pistol drop back into the holster.

Somebody laughed.

Likely it was no more than a release of tension, but it had a bad effect on Springer. His head whipped about in search of the one who had mocked him, and he glared terribly when he failed to single out a target—whoever laughed had managed to cover his mistake in time. Frustrated on all counts, humiliated, Reub Springer shot a last baleful look at the stranger. After that he swung his meaty shoulders and went tramping off across the street at a slant toward the nearest open saloon. And he went alone, even his friends seeming a little slow to follow.

The stranger watched him go and then turned again to Kit. His expression was bleakly sober. "I'll have to thank you for singing out," he said. "That was quick thinking."

She was having trouble with her own breathing. "He might have *killed* you! I actually thought he was going to try!"

"Seems a dumb sort of thing to be the cause of a shooting. I wonder if he ain't just a little crazy!"

"You wouldn't be the first to think it," she said. "Reub Springer is a bully, especially when he's been drinking, and I've always heard that he can't stand to be crossed. But he's smart about cattle and such things; and he must make a good range boss or surely Mr. Luft wouldn't keep him on."

The knot of bystanders was beginning to break up. The horses were growing restless on their towrope. The man appeared very much disturbed at what had happened: he took the time to put a thoughtful look along both sides of the street, almost as though he were checking against some other source of danger.

Only after that did he lower the hammer of his gun and slide the weapon into its holster. He took up the reins.

She said quickly, "You were asking for Orin Tracy . . . I'm Kit Tracy—he's my grandpa."

"Oh?" The man looked at her with new interest, and something caused a corner of his mouth to lift, with a hint of humor that softened the dark cast of his face. "And is he really eighty years old?"

"Pretty near." She added, "Grandpa's not here right now. He rode up to the county seat at Fossil. We were expecting him this morning but he isn't back yet."

"I see . . . Well, my name's Bannon. I've got a note for him, about these horses—from a man named Cap Flynn." He brought the note from a shirt pocket and handed it down to her.

"How is Cap?"

"Limping. He hurt his leg. That's why I got the job delivering these animals. You'll find it all in the note."

Standing there in the sun she opened it and read the scrawled and wretchedly misspelled lines while he waited. "It says you're to have twenty dollars," she said finally, looking up. "All right, Mr. Bannon. Why don't you take the horses on down to the barn? Howie Whipple will give you a hand with them. I'll be along directly and get you your money."

"Much obliged," he said, and this time he actually nodded and touched a finger to his hat brim. He kicked the dun and once more got his reluctant charges into motion; and Kit, suddenly mindful of her Sunday dress, stepped back and drew her skirt out of the way. Still holding the Bible and the note from Cap Flynn, she stood a moment and watched him ride away from her—compact and well-built, easily filling the saddle, the black hair hanging unevenly above the collar of his denim jacket.

A strange man, she thought. A surly fellow—but no, that wasn't true; he had a trace of humor. Was there something else about him? Something that weighed heavily and made him search the streets of an unfamiliar town for danger . . . ?

She knew what her best friend, Addie Weiker, would have said. Always the romantic, Addie would insist that the way he stood up to Reub Springer—the way he handled that gun—he must be an outlaw, maybe a famous one. Or a gunfighter, even a killer! But Kit Tracy had her own instincts, and they would not let her accept that.

Not an outlaw—no. But someone who had been injured and turned secretive . . . someone with trouble dogging his footsteps! The mystery of him tugged at something deep in her.

Chapter 3

Howie Whipple turned out to be a gangling fellow of indeterminate age, shy of manner and with hands like knots of rope, who seemed constantly to be trying to tuck his chin behind his Adam's apple. It took an exasperating amount of explaining to get it through his yellow-thatched head just what was wanted, even when Bannon invoked the names of Cap Flynn and of his boss's granddaughter. Finally understanding, he opened the corral gate and helped chivvy the half-wild horses inside it. Some of them balked—they had seen enough of corrals to know they didn't like them. By the time the ropes were off, the horses yelled inside, and the gate swung shut behind them, Kit Tracy was there to peer excitedly through the bars; her color was high and her eyes shone.

"Just look at the black!" she said to Bannon as he came down from the saddle. She had to make herself heard above the snorting and trumpeting and the thunder of hooves that shook the ground as the animals frantically circled the pen and the dust rose. "That chest of his!—and the proud way he throws his head! With the right handling, he'll make somebody a fine horse!"

"You like horses, don't you?" Bannon suggested. He had to admit her heightened color and shining eyes made an attractive contrast to the formal purity of the dress that was so uncommonly out of place here.

"I love them! After all, I've been around them practically all my life."

"You'd better watch out for that dress," he suggested. "You'll get it ruined."

She looked down at herself, as though she had forgotten what she was wearing. Quickly her manner changed. She smoothed a hand across her skirt and as she turned away said, quite sedately, "When you're through here come to the office. I'll have your money ready."

"Thanks."

He found her waiting, seated primly at the battered rolltop desk that had a Prineville feedstore's calendar nailed on the wall above it. The room was small but neat, with bare walls and linoleum on the floor, a cot in one corner for the night hostler. An open window framed a view of willows growing along the creek, the rocky slope across the canyon, the deep blue sky shot with clouds. Kit had removed her bonnet and placed it with the Bible on the desk at her elbow and done something with the brown curls that had started to come undone in her excitement over the horses. She gave Bannon a nod as he hesitated in the doorway and said, "Come in," motioning to a chair beside the desk. He complied, a little reluctantly, aware of the dustiness of his own clothing. He dropped his hat on the floor as he sat down.

A couple of gold-backed ten-dollar bills were on the desk, waiting for him, and the note from Cap Flynn. The girl said, "I guess I'll have to ask you to write me a receipt. You can do it on that same paper and that should make everything clear enough for Grandpa's records." Bannon took the pen she offered and wrote briefly, signed it, and added the date—July 3, 1904. While she looked at what he had written, then folded the paper and put it away in a pigeonhole of the desk, he asked, out of politeness and curiosity, "How long has your grandfather had this business?"

"We came here," she said, "over fifteen years ago—from Corvallis, in the Valley. My people were all farmers, but Daddy was killed in an accident, clearing timber. And when Mama's lungs started giving her trouble, the doctors said the drier climate this side of the mountains might do her good. Turned out that it didn't help much—but by the time she died we were settled here and we just stayed on."

"You like it?"

She hesitated and answered indirectly. "I was a little girl. So this is the only home I really remember, and I've got nothing to compare it with. And what about you, Mr. Bannon?" she added. "Where are *you* from?"

"A good number of places. The Boise country, most recent." Not elaborating, he carefully folded the two bills and buttoned them into a pocket of his shirt. There was a moment's stillness, broken by sounds through the window—the whisper of the creek over its stony bed, the noise the horses made reluctantly settling to the confinement of their pen.

Kit Tracy said, in a musing tone, "I admit I've wondered what it would be like, to be moving around and seeing different things—not always stuck in one tiny place . . . Well, there ought to be excitement enough here tomorrow!" Her eyes lifted to the calendar above the desk, with its colored picture of an

D. B. Newton

unlikely-looking stag posing against improbable rocks and pine trees. "We make a big thing of the Fourth of July here, Mr. Bannon. People come in from fifty miles away—all over the range—just to help us celebrate."

"I sort of thought," he observed dryly, "some of those fellows up the street may have started their celebrating early!"

"Reub Springer and his friends!" She made a face. "I'm sure they started last night and plan to keep at it all through the Fourth! I would expect it from them—they're like a holdover from the way things used to be around here, in the old days.

"You might not believe it now, but there was a time—with the mines booming and the range opening up—when Mitchell had the name of being just about the wildest place in the state of Oregon! I don't remember it very well, but Grandma says she doesn't know how she had the nerve to stick it out. Things changed when the town government was organized, and we got a jail and a town marshal who wouldn't stand for any nonsense. It's all different now, though even today, matters can get out of hand sometimes—like on the Fourth of July."

"Then what do you do?"

"Oh, we don't let it bother us too much. We just stay inside and bolt the doors. If there's trouble, it happens in the saloons, down here in the canyon—in the old days they used to call this section 'Tiger Town'—I suppose because it's where the prospectors and buckaroos came to buck the tiger. Up on Piety Hill, where the church and the school and most of the houses are, we get some noise but usually that's about all."

Bannon said, "Well, I hope there won't be any

trouble tomorrow. I guess I won't be around to see it, if there is."

"You're not staying over?"

"I've got to get on. Those broncs lost me a lot of time—they just wouldn't cooperate. Gave me and the rope an argument every foot of the way, until I finally persuaded them." He leaned for the hat he'd dropped beside his chair. "Fifty miles to Prineville, I understand. I better find something to eat and be on my way."

"Why not eat with us, Mr. Bannon?" Kit Tracy suggested. "With my grandma and me."

He said quickly, "I couldn't do that."

She wore a tiny gold watch pinned to the front of her dress; she referred to it. "Church is nearly over—we always sit down to the table at twelve-thirty sharp. Everything's ready and keeping hot on the back of the stove, with Grandpa not back yet to help us eat it."

"But all I did was deliver a few horses," he protested. "I can't invite myself into your home—a total stranger!"

"You're not inviting yourself," she corrected him, as she pushed back her chair. "Grandma would be very much put out if she knew I didn't ask you. Besides, you won't find any decent eating places open along the street—so, it's all settled."

Apparently it was. On Kit's invitation he brought in the dun and watered it and put it into a stall, with a bait of grain against the work it still had to do that day. He took off his gun and belt and left them hanging on the saddle. Afterward, they left the stable in charge of Howie Whipple and put the creek to their backs as they crossed the wide roadway.

Bannon now learned that one reached the houses atop the bluff—Piety Hill—by way of a tributary gulch, over a steep wagon road the girl called Nelson Street. This was lined with more of the town's business houses, and just beyond a bulky square structure that housed the jail, a flight of wooden steps with a rickety handrail angled up the hill. Kit leading the way, they mounted these and at the top halted a moment to stand in the sun and wind, with the village at their feet.

Kit pointed out the landmarks: Bailey Butte, an eroded lava plug she said was a challenge to climb; below them, Bridge Creek flowing north to enter the John Day at a place that had been called Burnt Ranch ever since the Snake chief Paulina put it to the torch, shortly after the close of the Civil War. A rough country, Ed Bannon thought, with little beauty but a certain power to it. Aside from sparsely growing scrub, almost the only green he could see was in the willows along Bridge Creek, and the pines and Lombardy poplars and lush fruit trees that made this isolated canyon an oasis.

He asked the girl, "What other towns do you have around here?"

"None very close that amount to anything. Fossil's the county seat, and that's forty miles north across the John Day. It's fifty miles up to Antelope, in Wasco County between here and The Dalles. Of course there's Prineville, over west—it's about the same distance and you have to go through the Ochocos to get there."

"I wouldn't say you're exactly crowded, are you? Of course," he added, "I realize the important thing, in this kind of country, is water."

"We have plenty of that," Kit said. "Besides the

creek, there's springs flowing out of this canyon wall that have never been known to go dry. People live well here. Nearly everybody in town has a garden; we raise more fruit and vegetables than we can possibly eat.

"On the other hand, I guess it's possible to get too much water! Old-timers still talk about a flood they had here the year I was born—back in eighty-four." She pointed to the south end of the canyon where the willow-lined rush of the creek came into view around a turn. "Eight feet of water came pouring through during a storm—without any warning at all. It took out a lot of houses. Afterward the town had to be rebuilt."

"You mean to say, they went ahead and rebuilt it in the very same place?"

"What would you have them do? It was either that or pull stakes and leave. There just isn't any other place around here where you could put a town."

"I should think you'd be afraid what happened once could happen again."

"Well, it hasn't—not in twenty years." She smiled. "Don't worry, Mr. Bannon. I don't really intend to go floating off down to the ocean!" And then, with one of the swift changes of mood he had already detected in her, Kit's smile faded and when she spoke again, it was on a different, wistful note: "Though sometimes I have a feeling that could be the only way I ever will get to see it . . ."

Suddenly Bannon felt his mouth draw out and harden. It was as though her words had struck a remembered chord, responding with the sound of another woman's voice, another woman's words that lay in his mind like a weight of lead: *I'm being stifled! I've got to get out of this country, and this marriage.*

*Please help me, Ed, if you don't want to see me lose my
mind . . . oh God, help me! There's nothing I wouldn't do
to show my gratitude . . .*

He felt his hands drawn into fists. He became
aware that the girl had broken off whatever she was
saying, while she stared at him as though in recoil
from the thing she saw reflected in his face. Ed Bannon caught himself, but he could not quite control
his voice as he said lamely, "I'm sorry. I guess I wasn't
listening."

She actually appeared shaken. She stammered an
answer: "All I said was—we don't seem quite so isolated here, now that we've got the telephone."

That jarred through to him. "Telephone?"

She pointed out the line of poles that marched off
down the canyon, the single wire gleaming faintly
where sunlight fell upon it from a sky dotted with
fine-weather cumulus. "It was put in a couple of
years ago. There's only one instrument in town—at
the drugstore. But it does make us feel we aren't entirely cut off from the rest of the world."

"Where does the line run?" he wanted to know.

"As far as Antelope . . ."

Where, naturally, there'd be other connections,
he thought bleakly—to The Dalles, to Portland; to
Prineville, as like as not. This was something he
hadn't anticipated, and it filled him with dark misgivings. It could mean serious trouble.

The girl's behavior had changed completely, as
though to match his own. She turned away abruptly,
as she told him, "Maybe we'd better get along.
Grandma will be wondering where I am, especially
since I missed church . . ."

The house where the Tracys lived was small but
homelike behind its picket fence, the white clap-

board siding neatly painted, the adjoining garden showing it received its share of care and attention. The interior held the collected furnishings of a life-time without looking cluttered. When he saw Kit's grandmother, Bannon decided the house was a reflection of her personality—she, also, was a small and tidy person. And her resemblance to the girl was a little startling—she must have passed her looks down, intact, through her son to her granddaughter. It was like seeing a flash of how the younger woman would appear some fifty years or so later—the features past maturity, the hair gone white, but the brown eyes undimmed by time.

As the girl predicted, Mary Tracy had shown no hesitation over the invitation to dinner. One swift, appraising glance at the stranger, as the situation was explained to her, and she was nodding brightly and saying, "Why, of course, Mr. Bannon. You're more than welcome. Where would our manners be, if we was to let you ride away hungry? Katherine, you get to work now and set another place."

It was Kit herself who, from her almost angry expression as she turned away, Bannon might have thought was wishing she could rescind her invitation. He felt a pang of regret at his own behavior. A man, once badly stung, had an understandable right to his suspicions; but surely this time— He let the matter rest, unsettled, and asked Mary Tracy for soap and water and a towel. At a wash bench on the screened-in back porch he cleaned up as best he could, ran a comb through his black hair, knocked the dust from his clothing, and wiped his boots; afterward he felt halfway presentable enough to sit down to Sunday dinner at the immaculate, white-clothed table.

Dinner was a chicken from the Tracys' own hen-house, stewed with dumplings; succotash and carrots and potatoes from the Tracys' garden, and biscuits so light they seemed ready to float off the plate. Bannon had never eaten better and he said so. Kit, he noticed, maintained her silence at first but it seemed unnatural for her and presently she began to open up, especially when her grandmother showed an interest in the animals their guest had delivered. "Any likely horseflesh in the string, Mr. Bannon?" the old lady wanted to know.

Sensing that she had as much knowledge of such matters as her granddaughter, Ed Bannon answered seriously. "Nothing to startle you, except for one black stud—he has good lines and a lot of fight to him. If he can be gentled right and not simply broken, I think he has the makings of a real horse."

Kit was ready and eager to confirm that. "You *must* come down and have a look! It's a long time since we've had anything like him in the corral. I'm only hoping Grandpa will hold onto him until he finds the right buyer who'll see he's treated the way he should be."

"I'm sure you can trust your grandfather, Katherine," the older woman promised. "No man has a keener eye for a horse than Orin Tracy—not after a lifetime dealing in them."

"Your husband sounds like considerable of a man," Bannon commented, accepting a refill of his coffee cup. "I'm sorry I didn't get to meet him. I just hope there hasn't been any trouble."

"Oh, I don't think so. He has friends at Twickenham he likes to stop with on the way back from Fossil. He'll be showing up—it all depends what time he got started this morning. I know he'll be sorry," she went on, "to learn about Cap Flynn getting hurt. They're old friends. You say Cap shot himself in the leg? With his own gun?"

"Yes, ma'am. I don't think it's anything serious, but it's painful. He's going to have to take it easy awhile."

"Sounds about like something Cap Flynn would do," the old lady commented dryly. "And I can't see him taking it easy . . ."

Later, over cherry pie, Mary Tracy turned the talk to their guest. "You're going to Prineville, Mr. Bannon? Will you be staying on there?"

"No, ma'am." He busied himself with his fork as he gave her a careful answer. "I'm heading generally for California. San Francisco," he added, naming the first place that came to mind. "Fellow I know may have a job for me."

She made a clucking sound. "My! That *is* a long way . . . ! I visited San Francisco once—years ago. Really a big city now, I hear. I'm sure I could never hope to fit in anywhere like that. I love my little house and garden too much, and the sort of people who live in a place like Mitchell. Besides, travel's for young folks. Isn't that right, Katherine?"

The question brought Bannon's glance to the girl. She seemed in no hurry to answer her grandmother; head tilted to one side, Kit appeared to consider.

She said seriously, "Mr. Bannon and I were talking about that earlier. I do think about such things— quite a lot, sometimes. I know I'd love to make the trip Grandpa's talked about so much—to see the ocean, and Portland, and our old place in the Valley that I don't even really remember. I don't imagine, though, I'd be happy very far away from this part of Oregon—not for good. Of course, since I've never been anywhere else I can't really say. But I figure it's something I can worry about some other time."

All at once Ed Bannon felt a guilty crawling of shame. She was so plainly in earnest, he knew now he had misinterpreted what he had heard before; he had unintentionally done her a real wrong. Angry at himself, he put down his fork and pushed his plate away. He heard the gruffness in his own voice as he said, "Speaking of time, I'm using up too much of yours. I'll never get on the road if I sit here talking all afternoon." He rose abruptly. "Thank you, Mrs. Tracy," he told the older woman. "It was a dandy meal . . ."

Afterward, ready to leave, he lingered a moment on the neat front porch, before making his way back down the hill to the livery where the dun waited in its stall. Kit had stepped outside with him. She stood against the railing and smoothed back the brown hair that the canyon breeze tried to whip from beneath her restraining hand. Her eyes were troubled. It seemed to take an effort for her to ask suddenly, "Did I say something earlier to make you angry? If I did, I'm sorry—even though I don't know what it was."

She was serious, and he answered her as seriously. "No, Kit. I'm the one should apologize. I let something bother me when I shouldn't have."

"But it *was* something I said?"

"Not you—somebody else." He shrugged slightly. "It really isn't worth discussing. It's just that—well, a man who's let himself be used can be pretty damned touchy about ever letting it happen again!"

The girl was studying his face, frowning like someone attempting to read a troubling riddle. "You thought I was trying to *use* you?"

Bannon shook his head emphatically. "You wouldn't. There ain't that kind of guile in you. I'm sure of it now, supposing I had doubts a little earlier. Sometimes it just ain't all that easy to be sure, even when you might think you have a person figured out."

"Like—the one we're talking about? . . . I think you must have been very badly hurt!"

"It don't matter," he said, a little roughly. "But, thanks for understanding." He added, "And for everything else—not least, for speaking up and keeping that fellow Springer from getting the deadwood on me, there on the street this morning. I just hope you won't have any trouble over that."

"With Reub Springer?" She gave her head a toss, the brown curls bouncing. "Pooh! I'm not afraid of *him*," she said, with a spirit that made Ed Bannon smile.

"Glad to hear it!" he said. "Right now it's time I was moving along. I'll be thinking about you tomorrow—hoping you're having a real good Fourth of July." He held out his hand.

Kit Tracy's smaller hand had a strong and forthright grip that was almost like a boy's. "Thank you," she said, the sunlight striking across her pleasant features. "And I'll—"

She didn't finish. Bannon, trained to wariness, had noticed the men before they reached the gate in the picket fence. Perhaps the girl caught his sudden tensing and the turn of his head; at the faint creak of the gate's inward swing she broke off, flashing him a last troubled glance before turning to see who was coming up the path.

Bannon was already facing them, conscious of the gun and belt he had left on his saddle at the stable.

For as one of the pair came up, swinging his arms to his restless stride, there was a brief flash of metal in the gap of the unbuttoned corduroy jacket—sunlight, bouncing off the polished tin of a badge pinned to his shirtfront. The second man was Howie Whipple, the stable hand, and he it was who said to his companion, in a voice turned hoarse with excitement, "That's him, Marshal. That's the fella!"

It was as though Bannon felt something turn over and settle like a clot of ice inside him.

Chapter 4

"What is it, Sam?" Kit Tracy wanted to know. "Has there been some trouble?" And to Bannon she explained quickly, "This is Sam Prentiss—our marshal."

Prentiss would be nearing sixty, a quick and energetic man with sharp blue eyes, and a skin so lined and pitted no razor could reach all the stubbles of beard. Like the thick mop of hair showing beneath the brim of his hat, his beard was only faintly shot with gray.

Bannon could feel the lawman's stare under the shadow of the brim, studying him and expertly sizing him up. The marshal said crisply, "And your name?" Ed Bannon gave it, with some reluctance, and the lawman said, "I understand you brought some horses in this morning."

"That's right. My orders were to turn them in at the livery."

"Where did you get them?"

This was going off in a direction Bannon hadn't been expecting; the persistent questioning puzzled him and angered him a little, too. He replied shortly, "From a man named Flynn. I don't know him, but he hired me to make the delivery."

"It would appear there's some question about that."

Kit had been growing more perturbed with every

moment. Now she exploded: "Sam, there *couldn't* be! Mr. Bannon brought us a note from Cap Flynn. Cap hurt his leg and couldn't deliver the horses himself . . ."

Howie Whipple, too, could contain himself no longer. Before the marshal could answer he impulsively broke in: "It's Reub Springer, Kit. Him and some others come down to the barn a while ago. Reub was talking loud about us having a horse in our corral that belonged to him—he meant the black stud we put there this morning. I tried to argue, but he wouldn't listen. He dabbed a rope on the black and led him out. Just helped himself!"

The door to the house had opened while he was talking and Mary Tracy, drawn by the excited voices, came out to join her granddaughter on the steps. She exclaimed, "Reub Springer did that?"

"Yes, ma'am."

The old lady clucked in disbelief. "He's *such* a troublemaker, especially when he's been drinking! I swear, sometimes I can't see why John Luft puts up with him."

"Well, the rest of 'em were all pretty drunk and egging him on. Maybe I should of tried to stop him," the hostler added. "But I'll admit Reub scares me when he's like that!"

"You did right," Kit Tracy assured him. "You aren't being paid to stand up to some drunken bully and risk getting seriously hurt! But what did he do after he took the black?"

"Rode on down the canyon, leading it on his rope. Said he was taking it home and nobody had better get any ideas about following him. One of them no-good friends of his rode along; the rest went back up the street—I guess to get on with their drinkin'."

"Home . . . ," she repeated. "He meant the JL?"

"I figure. Anyway, soon as he was gone I went looking for the marshal."

The lawman, frowning, was rubbing his stubbled chin with a fist. "Well," he said, "looks like I better ride out there and have a talk with Luft. As a town officer I got no jurisdiction at the JL, of course, but I can give him to understand his man has gone too far this time. Kit, did you say there's a note from Flynn?"

"It's in the desk at the office—you're welcome to take it. If you need someone along to identify the black, give me time to change my clothes and I'll ride with you."

But Mary Tracy had something to say about that. "No you won't!" she stated firmly. "I won't have you anywhere around when Reub Springer is making trouble!"

Kit protested. "Sam and Mr. Luft will see that he doesn't."

But the old lady was adamant, and Sam Prentiss agreed with her. "Your grandma's right, Kit. I won't need any help, I reckon, making Luft listen to me."

The girl wanted to argue but she broke off when she saw they were both set against her. "Oh, well—all right!"

Watching all this, apparently forgotten by the others, Ed Bannon was aware of an unwelcome suspicion hardening to a certainty. With it, came a growing conviction as to what he was going to have to do. It really seemed to leave him no choice. He let his shoulders settle and, reluctantly, asked the marshal, "Just how far is it to this JL?"

If Prentiss was surprised at the question, he didn't let it show. "How far? I dunno—six or seven miles, I guess. It's off the stage road to Prineville."

"Why, then"—Bannon spread his hands—"it's practically on my way. That being the case, I'll ride along with you, Marshal. I can point out the horse and tell your man Luft anything he needs to know. That shouldn't take too much time."

Sam Prentiss studied the stranger a long moment. He appeared to debate the offer, as though testing the stranger's motives. He said finally, "If you're sure you want to bother . . ."

"No bother."

"All right. I'll get my horse, Bannon, and meet you at the stable."

He was gone then, at a quick and nervous stride, with Howie Whipple following. Bannon turned to find Kit Tracy frowning at him. She said, "I do hope you won't be getting into any trouble, after what almost happened already between you and Reub Springer."

"No reason to expect it," he assured her, with a certainty he was a good way from feeling. "Even Springer will have to behave himself, with his boss and a lawman both looking on. And I was riding that direction anyhow." He took off his hat and offered his hand, first to the older woman and then to the younger one. "We've already said goodbye, and I've thanked you for that fine dinner. I guess I shouldn't keep your marshal waiting."

There seemed nothing to hold him. The last impression he had, as he pulled on his sweated range hat and turned away, was of Kit Tracy's troubled look— almost as though she knew there was something more in his mind than he was telling. Well, there was no reason for her to concern herself. It should be clear to her that he wasn't likely to pass this way again.

He swung the gate open, caught it with his heel as

it swung closed behind him. Not looking back, he headed for the wooden steps that would take him to the lower town and to the stable where his horse and gun were waiting for him.

The marshal rode a horse that was somehow like himself—a leggy, rawboned animal, a roan, with a nervous quickness about its movements and an intelligence in its rolling eye that seemed almost human. Mount and owner appeared to understand one another, so that Sam Prentiss hardly needed to convey an order to his mount except by some subtle touch of hand or pressure of knee. He was already in the saddle and waiting when Ed Bannon came down off the hill; Bannon saw that he had Cap Flynn's note from the desk in the office and appeared to be studying it, comparing the descriptions in the mustanger's scrawled writing with the animals nervously occupying the corral. He went on with this as Bannon fetched his own horse out of its stall. When Bannon emerged, the dun saddled and ready to ride, Prentiss folded the paper and shoved it away in a pocket of his corduroy coat.

If he noticed the revolver and cartridge belt, in place now about the stranger's middle, he made no comment. The marshal had armed himself with a belt gun and a carbine on his saddle—though Prentiss had more or less made light of this mission in front of the women, it was plain he believed in coming prepared.

No one watched them leave except for Howie Whipple, standing with his hands in the hip pockets of his manure-spattered overalls as the riders headed off down the canyon. They took a shallow fording of the creek, and there were a few more buildings. Bannon turned for a final look behind him at the town crowded onto the flat beside the creek, the houses up on the bench, the poplars and willows and fruit trees that made this a spot of lushness in a tortured landscape. He looked for the Tracy house but couldn't find it, though he saw the white church spire; it recalled what Kit had told him of the history of Piety Hill and Tiger Town.

Sam Prentiss spoke. "Not a bad little place, you know. Good climate, friendly people. And we'll never be crowded, the way it's getting over around Portland! I've been here nigh on thirty years, myself. Don't think I'd care to live anywhere else."

"Thirty years . . . then you must have been around for the flood."

"You heard about that, did you?" The marshal shrugged. "Yeah, it was quite a thing—took out a big hunk of the town. Further downcreek, in the Painted Hills country, a whole family got themselves drowned . . . Well, that was a long time back."

"Twenty years ain't very long. Because you've had one disaster with the creek don't mean you can't have another. Maybe you're overdue."

"Oh, we don't lose sight of that," Sam Prentiss said. "Any time those black thunderheads build and start moving south, toward the hills where these cricks head up, a lot of us still half expect a cloud-burst to break over there and send a waterspout whooping down the canyon."

Bannon had never heard a flash flood called a "waterspout," but he supposed it was a localism of back-country Oregon. He said, as he took up the reins, "One of these days it could happen."

"We figure we'll know in time to get out of the way."

You hope, Bannon thought, but didn't say it. And then the trail along Bridge Creek took a rocky turn and Mitchell was left behind them.

They rode on through a landscape of spires and plugs and ridges crusted with lava. Cloud shadows spotted the tawny hills. Aside from the steady hum of wind, the silence was almost a tangible thing. A hawk, circling on thermal updrafts against the broken sky, was almost the only living thing they saw.

"Rugged country," Ed Bannon commented.

The older man admitted it. "I remember one fellow saying it looked like hell with the fire out. Well, I guess at that we had plenty of fire, one time. This is all volcanic country—hot lava and ashes, laid down when the Cascades over west of us was blowing off. Had a college professor come through, some years back—he told me this was all swamp and tropical forest a long time ago, before the climate changed. Showed me some fossils he'd been digging up, back in the John Day breaks—petrified pieces of mammoths, and camels even, and things he called 'sabertooth tigers'—damnedest stuff I ever seen! I can tell you, after hearing him, the place never looked quite the same to me again . . ."

Bannon listened to the marshal talk, not offering much comment, letting the man's voice break the monotony of their riding. Presently they reached a place where the road forked. A tributary entered Bridge Creek at this point, from the west; they turned aside here into another wagon track that, Sam Prentiss said, would take Bannon up this smaller stream and over the hump of the Ochocos, and so down to Prineville.

It was while they paused to breathe and water their horses, the silence of the empty land pressing around them, that the marshal suddenly asked, "When are you going to tell me what really decided you to take this ride?"

Bannon looked at him, meeting the blue stare that almost seemed to jab at him with barbed edges. Keeping his own voice without expression, he said, "I don't think I know what you mean."

The marshal had dug up a smoke-blackened pipe from somewhere and seemed to be debating whether to fill and fire it up. Turning it in his hand he said, "You don't fool me too much. I was watching you and I seen your face when you made up your mind. What I want to know is why?" His stare lifted directly to the stranger. "Understand, I don't figure I'll be seeing you again, once this little matter is settled and you ride on your way. I ain't asked you any questions about things that don't concern me. But this is one question I think I got a right to ask."

Bannon nodded. "That makes sense. All right. I'm going with you because I don't have any choice. Unless I'm mistaken, Springer's taking the black was aimed at me."

"At *you?*" the marshal snapped. "How does that figure?"

"I don't believe anyone mentioned that I had a little trouble with Reub Springer this morning, when I first hit town with those horses. Just to test me, he tried to lay claim to the black, and I bluffed him out. I thought that would be the end of it; but now he's thrown me a challenge and he's daring me to rise to it. I can hardly back away."

"I see." At the moment, the marshal's pitted, stubbled cheeks could have been cast from bronze. "Had I known all this, I might not have took up your offer quite so quick."

"Maybe that's the reason I didn't tell you."

Sam Prentiss let out his breath with a snort. He apparently decided against the pipe and shoved it back into a pocket of the corduroy jacket. He said heavily, "You're probably just imagining it. Reub Springer seen a horse he liked and helped himself. Doesn't have to have anything to do with you at all."

"Maybe," Bannon said. "I dare say we'll find out . . ."

A pair of wagon ruts took off to the south, crossing the tributary, and here Sam Prentiss turned aside into what seemed the approach to John Luft's spread. The wagon tracks took a twisting course through the lava outcrops and bunchgrass flats and scrub junipers. "Luft's got him a pretty fair operation here," the marshal said. "By a long way, the biggest one around. He owns a lot of acres, has a good balance of water and grass, and reserve and timber pasture. Ships a big beef crop, hires a big crew—and incidentally, gives Mitchell a good-sized amount of trade. Don't really know what the town would do without him."

"So in other words," Bannon interpreted in a dry tone, "he carries weight. And expects—and gets— special treatment."

"That's how the world operates," Sam Prentiss said, with a shrug.

Once Ed Bannon pointed to the horse sign they had been following; its meaning was unmistakable, the droppings and the marks of the hooves less than an hour old. One set—those of Reub Springer's saddle horse—had been made by steel shoes; the barefoot prints of the black, following on the rope, were all over the road.

"He's still fighting," Bannon pointed out. "He

fought me all the way from Cap Flynn's dugout, and he isn't any closer yet to quitting."

Prentiss wagged his grizzled head in appreciation. "I want to see that horse!"

"Tell you what I wouldn't want to see—it's a spirit like that, broken."

"At the hands of Reub Springer, you mean." The marshal gave him a look; the look turned speculative and he suggested, "You could do the job better yourself? You've had experience handling the wild ones, maybe?"

"Some," Bannon admitted shortly, and something in his tone seemed to warn the lawman he was asking the questions he had indicated he would not. Prentiss let the matter drop.

Presently the wagon ruts snaked down through a shallow pass and all at once John Luft's ranch headquarters lay before them.

This was a natural setting, with glint of water and some cottonwoods and pines, and a stretch of pretty good hay pasture under wire. Bannon was surprised, though, at the ranch layout: for a man who, from all report, appeared to be doing well enough for himself, it didn't strike him this John Luft lived in any great style. The barn and other work buildings looked in good enough shape, but the sprawling house had been a long time without paint and the yard around it held unnecessary trash and the shine of freshly discarded tin cans. He saw no bunkhouse; he wondered if Luft shared the house with his crew, bachelor fashion. If so, judging from the exterior, the inside of the house would actually be something of a rat's nest.

And then, holding to a walk as they rode on toward the cluster of buildings, they saw the black.

It stood beside an empty corral, snubbed to a post

by the towrope that had led it here. Its head hung, and its hide was gray with the dust plastered there by the lather of its exertions. Otherwise, at first glance, the yard in the vicinity of the ranch house and barn seemed empty of life or of any movement except for the slow shuttering and flow of cloud shadows pushed by a warm wind.

Bannon heard the marshal's grunt as he saw the horse and said, "Yes, there's the bait. Springer put it here for me and he's waiting to see if I'll rise to it. Or, maybe you're still unconvinced?"

Sam Prentiss had no comment.

They rode on in, across a narrow bridge of juniper logs that spanned a dry wash, and reined in for a closer look at the black. Its head was up now, the intelligent eyes watching them warily, and it moved away as far as the snubbed rope would allow it. For all it had undergone, the black was no nearer ready to accept being a captive.

Dust blew up grittily and was swept away on the ground breeze. And now both men turned, without dismounting, as something moved in the flickering shade of a cottonwood. A pair of men had been seated there on a rough wooden bench, obviously waiting—one was Reub Springer and Bannon thought he recognized the other, from that scene on the street earlier in the day, as one of Springer's friends. Now the range boss got to his feet and walked out from under the tree shadow, a hulking and formidable shape. His stare touched both riders and then settled on Ed Bannon. He said roughly, "So—you brought the law, did you?"

It was Prentiss who answered. "The other way around. I was coming; he happened to be on his way to Prineville and offered to ride this far with me."

At this the big man's aggressive stare switched to the marshal. He showed the first trace of uncertainty. "We ain't in town, Prentiss. What the hell business would you have here?"

"I think I should discuss that with your boss. Is he around?"

As he was speaking, a screen door squealed on its hinges and now a voice said, "Over here, Prentiss." A man came out onto the steps of the house. Ed Bannon gave the dun a touch with his knee that moved it around so that he could get a look at this John Luft without at the same time losing sight of Springer.

The JL owner came down the steps and approached them. He could have been forty. He had the kind of face that can be strong enough to make up for what it lacks in handsomeness. The intelligent look of the wide-spaced brown eyes and a firmness about the shape of the mouth gave Luft an air of considerable personal power—an ability to issue orders and expect them to be obeyed. Still, something troubled Bannon; and now, as the screen banged open again and a straggle of men followed their boss down the steps into the yard, he suspected that he knew what it was.

In his time Ed Bannon had worked on occasion for unmarried ranchers who, dispensing with a separate bunkhouse, simply shacked with their crews, and he had usually found it was hard to tell the employer from the hands. So it was here. John Luft allowed himself a strain of coarseness, almost a slovenliness, that failed to distinguish him from the ordinary buckaroos on his payroll. And to a man of Ed Bannon's temperament, that was entirely improper.

John Luft might be a successful rancher and a powerful man, but he lacked quality.

He came to a halt now, looking from his range boss to the pair of riders, and he settled on Sam Prentiss. "What's going on?" he demanded.

The marshal explained without preliminary. "Reub Springer here helped himself to a bronc out of Tracy's corral in town—claimed it was his. I got a piece of paper that says different. Orin being away, I volunteered to try and get it straightened out."

Luft scowled and held out a hand. "Let's see the paper." Prentiss passed it down, and as the rancher studied it Ed Bannon gave a glance to Reub Springer. The big man was frowning, chewing at the inside of his lower lip. He looked bothered; Bannon had an impression this thing was taking a turn Springer hadn't counted on.

Luft raised his eyes from the paper to the black tied at the corral post. "Is this the horse?"

Prentiss nodded, and Ed Bannon said, "I delivered it this morning, along with some others. Bannon's the name."

Luft had already checked that against the signature on the receipt. He said, "And you're positive it's the same horse?"

"No question about it."

Fuming, Reub Springer broke in. "It makes no difference what anybody says or what's written on some piece of paper! I claim the stud."

"On what grounds?" his boss wanted to know.

"Prior ownership. He was a wild bronc and I caught him—and he still belongs to me, whatever this bastard says!"

"Not if you couldn't hang on to him," Sam Prentiss commented. "Supposing you ever had him, looks like he got away and gone wild again. That made him fair game for Flynn or anybody else."

"The hell it did! He was part of my string, I tell you."

John Luft's thoughtful stare rested on his range boss now. "Just where was it you caught him?"

"Over near French Peak," the big man promptly answered. "When I was holding down the camp there last year."

"If he was part of your string, seems funny I don't remember ever seeing you ride him. What about the rest of you boys?" Luft threw the question to the half dozen JL hands standing by. Ed Bannon could see that it put them on the spot. One or two shifted their boots and cast uneasy looks at the big range boss—under the threat in his black stare, it was plain they were unwilling to back up his claim with a lie, yet were afraid of the consequences if they didn't.

Bannon became impatient. "Can't we cut this short?" he said. "All anybody has to do is take a look at the black. That animal has never been shod, and he's never been worked. Ain't a spur or saddle mark on him—which there certainly would be, if Springer had ever been on top of him wearing *those* hooks!" He pointed to the cruel barbs that were, even now, strapped to the man's scuffed cowhides. "Isn't that proof enough that he's lying?"

Springer's head snapped up; his chest swelled with temper. "Here, now! By God—"

His employer cut him off, saying roughly, "It would appear he made a mistake, anyway." The rancher was a man of sudden decisions; abruptly he handed the marshal back his paper and told him, "Go ahead, then. Take the black."

"Thanks for being reasonable." But though he had what he'd come for, the older man seemed reluctant to close the matter there. "By rights," he pointed out, "I ought to take Springer too, for stealing him . . ."

"Oh, no! You needn't think I'd let you have my range boss, because of some penny-ante doings in that town of yours!" John Luft firmly shook his head. "Back off, Sam! I'm giving you the horse—don't push for more."

Bannon had a feeling that Sam Prentiss took real pride in the badge he wore; this kind of arrogance must be hard for him to swallow. But against the power of a wealthy rancher, his small-town marshal's post gave him no actual authority and he knew it. The bitter knowledge showed in his eyes and in the sour twist of his mouth. Giving up the argument, he turned to the black horse—and at once, as though understanding what was coming, the stud laid back his ears and rolled an eye at him in warning.

Ed Bannon broke in quietly, "I'll take charge of the black. I've learned something about him." And he kneed the dun forward.

"*No!*" Reub Springer had been driven past endurance. As Bannon reached for the halter rope, the black stud raising dust and trying to evade him, there was a flash of metal. A gun leaped into Springer's big fist and he fired, without warning, directly into that confusion of men and horses at the corral fence. It had to be an unthoughtful gesture of pure frustration. Bannon had no idea where the bullet might have gone to, but he never doubted it had been meant for him. Turned coldly furious, he forgot the black and instead gave his horse a kick that jumped it straight at the man with the smoking gun. His own revolver swept from the holster, and as he settled the startled dun, he aimed the handgun straight at Springer's face.

"All right!" he cried harshly. There was a good deal of angry frustration in Ed Bannon, too, just then. His finger ached with an impulse to pull the trigger, but he held it in check even as he curbed the dun on tight-drawn rein.

Reub Springer, though, must have read something in the face that glared at him down the barrel of the gun. He seemed to forget the smoking weapon in his own hand; he gave back a step, and some of the whiskey shine left his staring eyes.

Bannon would not let up. "I guess we both know why it really was you took that animal! You've just been spoiling for a fight with me, Springer—and I'm in the mood to give you one! So, either use that gun you're holding or drop it! Damn you, make up your mind!"

Reub Springer was already rattled enough at the cruel way his plan had gone wrong. Now, with the stranger crowding him, he seemed unable to pull his thoughts together. His battered face looked blotched and his eyes muddied; his fist began to tremble and he opened it and let the gun hit the dirt in front of his boots.

But there was no way he could accept being humiliated in front of his employer and the rest of the crew—to say nothing of the crony he had brought from town to see him handle Bannon and who was staring, open-mouthed, aghast at the way things were turning out. "Next time—," Reub Springer began hoarsely.

"Don't count on a next time," Bannon advised him. "I'm only passing through, remember? You've had all the chance at me you're likely to get." And with that he pulled the dun around, deliberately turning his back on Springer while he looked for John Luft and the other JL men.

There didn't appear to be any danger from that quarter. No one had moved. He didn't see any weapons or sign of anyone taking up the fight for the big range boss. Bannon lowered the hammer of his gun off cock and returned it to the holster. As he did, John Luft said in a voice as frigid as ice, "I told you once before—take that horse and get the hell out of here!"

Bannon looked to Sam Prentiss for his cue. The marshal was stangely white of face, as though with shock at what might have happened here. He didn't try to speak but merely nodded; actually there seemed no further point in talking. Bannon reached and jerked free the rope that held the black stud to the corral post and, in a continuing silence, turned away without looking again at Luft or any of his men. Ed Bannon sent his dun horse after the marshal's. They clattered across the narrow bridge, and were gone.

Chapter 5

They could not have ridden far when Sam Prentiss said, in an odd voice, "Maybe we better hold up a minute . . ."

Bannon had been dividing his attention between his animals and watching the back trail, in case Reub Springer might decide to make another try. He glanced quickly at the marshal and, for the first time, noticed his pallor and the sweat that gleamed wetly on his face. Sam Prentiss had let his animal drift to a halt, and now Bannon saw him withdraw a hand from the gap of his corduroy jacket. The fingers were smeared with crimson.

Ed Bannon swore, remembering as he did the wild shot from Springer's gun that had narrowly missed him back there in the JL yard. It looked as though the bullet had found a target, quite by accident. Sam Prentiss sat motionless, staring as though mesmerized by the sight of his own blood. Hastily Bannon reined over, pulled Prentiss' jacket aside and revealed the red stain already spreading through the material of the marshal's shirt. He said sternly, "Man, you should have spoke up—let that fellow Luft know about this and see that he did something."

But the lawman shook his head. "No!" he said through lips that were tight with pain. "We had to get away from there! That crazy Reub Springer—I wasn't sure Luft could keep a rein on him if we didn't get out, quick!" He shifted position, and his leathery face broke up in a grimace of pain. "Take off my gun belt, will you? It drags a mite."

Quickly Bannon complied, refastened the buckle, and hung belt and gun on the marshal's saddle horn. But then he said, "You can't ride this way. You're bleeding like a stuck hog!"

For answer, Sam Prentiss fumbled and brought out a handkerchief from his pocket, wadded it, and placed it inside his shirt. Bannon insisted, "That's not going to do a lot of good. You got to have a doctor."

"I'll last, I reckon," the marshal said gruffly, "till I reach town." He straightened like a man exerting the force of his will. The hand he reached toward Bannon shook a little. "Pass me the rope," he said. "I'll take the black and be getting along . . ."

Ed Bannon looked at the hand, at the face that was drained of color and the eyes dulled with shock. "No," he said. "I don't think you're up to handling him. You go on. Ride ahead—I'll follow with the black."

The lawman tried to protest, but in the end he could only nod and give his mount a nudge with one heel that started it forward again. Anxiously watching the sag of the man's shoulders, Ed Bannon again took up the rear.

At the creek he got down and, while the marshal clung to his place in the saddle, had a closer look at the wound. It was hard to tell how serious it might be. The bullet had drilled an irregular hole, tearing the flesh as it exited—the wonder had to be that Sam Prentiss wasn't thrown from his saddle when it hit him. Bannon ripped up a clean shirt from his saddlebags and bathed the wound with water from the creek. He thought the bleeding appeared to have slacked off somewhat, which was a good sign. He made a compress from one of the sleeves—the marshal said, "I owe you for the shirt," but Bannon let that pass without comment.

He said, "If you start feeling light-headed, grab for the saddle horn—I might not be able to reach you to save you from a spill."

For a long moment the other man looked down at him from the saddle. "Looks like I may have figured you wrong, Bannon," he said finally. "Something about you still bothers me—you'd like folks to think you're an ordinary sort of fiddle foot, but I don't believe that for a minute. Still, you ain't as hard as I took you to be at first sight, either. A man has to have a heart in him somewhere, to take this much trouble."

Hearing that, Ed Bannon let the mask drop into place. His face expressionless, a hint of deep bitterness coloring his voice, he said curtly, "Don't always bet on what somebody's got in him!" And leaving the other man to puzzle over that if he wanted to, he turned to seek his own saddle and take the lead rope of the black.

Ed Bannon was in no mood for taking nonsense from the black, which had already caused far more inconvenience than Bannon ever reckoned on when he made his bargain with Cap Flynn. Perhaps by now the horse knew him well enough to be wary of him, for this time the stud put up no great fight against the lead rope and it was only concern for Sam Prentiss' hurt that slowed them down on the ride back to Mitchell.

Late shadows were building in the canyon as they reentered this town Bannon had not expected to see again. They turned in at the stable and Howie Whipple came out to meet them, trailed by a couple of the town loafers for whom the livery was apparently a favorite hangout. Bannon didn't say much nor answer many of their questions as he turned the black into the corral; but he had no doubt that garbled rumors of what had happened out at Luft's would soon be spreading through the village.

It didn't much interest him. He was concerned only about the marshal, who rode slumped in the saddle with his boots slogged deep into the stirrups and said nothing at all. Bannon had already inquired from him how to find the doctor's house; without dismounting now he said, "Let's go get that bullet hole tended to."

Doc Ashby was one who didn't live up on Piety Hill. Probably to be handy for emergencies, he had a small frame shack near the hotel, set back from the street with the canyon wall just behind; it was flanked by a garden almost choked with melons, squash, corn, and tomatoes ripening on the vine— thanks to ever-flowing springs and the climate of this pleasant, sheltered place, almost anything seemed to grow here. Ashby, a bachelor in his thirties, was at work in the garden when the two men rode up. He left his hoe leaning against a fence post and came to meet them, brushing loose dirt from his hands.

He was the type that goes bald early—a tall man, clean-shaven, with a wedge-shaped face that widened at the hinges of the jaw, and a brisk manner of moving and speaking. He took one look at the injured man and said simply, "All right, let's get him down from there."

They did it, between them. Sam Prentiss got his right leg free of the stirrup and swung it over his horse's back. But when his boots touched the ground, his knees sagged and he would have gone on down, except that Bannon caught him and slipped the man's left arm across his shoulders. Supporting his weight, the two half walked and half carried him into the house, Ed Bannon with the marshal's gun belt looped over one arm.

Ashby's furniture was mostly pickups, with nothing matching anything else and most of it rather shabby as though he was careless as to where and how he lived. But an inner door opened on a consulting room that was spotless and gleamed with the instruments of his trade. They took the hurt man in there and got him up on the operating table. Bannon found a chairback to hang the belt on, and then stood watching while the doctor, having washed up and rolled his sleeves, set to work stripping the injured man of coat and shirt. As he exposed the makeshift, bloody bandage, the doctor asked crisply, "Who shot him?"

"Fellow named Springer."

"Springer . . ." The doctor spoke the name in a tone of heavy distaste. "I can't say I'm surprised."

"It was an accident."

"Accident!" In the same scornful tone.

"That's right," Bannon said. "He was trying to shoot *me*."

He caught the sharp edge of the look that remark got him, but Ashby had no more questions as he cleaned the wound and studied the damage from the bullet. He said presently, "I hope you don't mind the sight of blood."

Bannon, examining the penmanship of a framed

diploma from a medical school in Ohio, told him, "I can't say I'm partial to it—but I've seen quite a lot of his, by now."

"Afraid you're apt to see some more of it." He explained: "You understand what we've got here. The bullet should have made a good, clean hole. Instead, it was deflected by a rib and probably cracked it. Just to be sure, I'm going to have to do some probing for bone splinters." Doc Ashby tossed aside the cloth he'd dried his hands on, and brought a metal tray of wicked-looking instruments from a cabinet. "He seems to be out cold, so I'll go ahead and work on him. But I need somebody to hold him quiet in case he starts to move around. I guess you're elected."

Ed Bannon nodded reluctantly. "All right."

He had never thought of himself as squeamish, but there was something about the long steel probe, deliberately entering the bullet's channel and searching around in there, that threatened to undo him. He felt the heat in his throat and swallowed a number of times against the sour pressure he could feel rising. As he watched, he wondered how Ashby could perform his task so coolly, with no more emotion than a sober concentration. Once, under Bannon's hands, the unconscious man gave a jerk of suddenly tensed muscles and the faintest of groans.

But finally the doctor uttered a grunt of satisfaction, withdrew the bloody piece of steel and tossed it back onto the tray with a clatter. "The rib seems to be all right," he pronounced. "And no apparent damage to the lung. Looks like Sam Prentiss is in luck. . . . I can finish up here," he added, as a shrewd look at Bannon showed him something in his helper's face. "Why don't you step outside and have a smoke?"

Bannon admitted gruffly, "I could use the smoke . . ."

The cigarette helped. It was half-finished and his stomach had settled and his hands lost their foolish shaking, when the doctor came out upon the porch where he was seated on the railing, listening to the small sounds of the village. Doc Ashby seemed surprised to see him. "I sort of thought you'd of taken off."

"I wanted at least to know how he came through."

"Your name Bannon?" And at the other's nod: "Then he wants to see you."

A trifle puzzled, Bannon shrugged and nodded as he tossed the butt of his cigarette across the rail.

Ashby took him through the consulting room to another one behind it—the house was larger than it looked from outside. This room contained a couple of beds and very little else; one of the beds held Sam Prentiss. The doctor ushered Bannon inside and then closed the door, leaving him alone with the hurt man. Either Ashby had no natural curiosity or his job had trained him to mind his own business.

Prentiss lay partly on his back and partly on his left side, with pillows arranged to support the wound as comfortably as could be done. Bannon thought he looked ten years older than when he set out for Luft's only a few hours ago. His face appeared white and waxen and somehow fallen in on itself. The bullet wound and the loss of blood had obviously hit him hard.

He looked at Bannon, standing in the doorway. He said, "I still owe you for that shirt I ruined."

Bannon said, "Forget the shirt."

"All right, then. I owe you for bringing me in to

the doc. By now you could have been well on your way to Prineville."

"That's so," Bannon agreed noncommittally. He changed the subject. "How are you feeling?"

Instead of answering, the injured man tried to twist about for a look at the small deal table that stood by the bed. "Do you see any water there?" It held a tumbler and a china pitcher. Bannon stepped over and poured a glassful, but when the marshal reached for it his hand trembled so that the younger man had to steady it while he drank.

Sam Prentiss sank back, gasping. "Thing like this can really give a man a thirst," he said as Bannon replaced the glass on the table. He went on, moving his head against the pillow, "It's sure a helluva note, to be laid up this way! Doc says it could be weeks before I'm good for anything. Meantime, I guess I don't have to remind anybody what day it is tomorrow—besides being Monday."

Actually, Bannon had almost forgotten his earlier discussion with Kit Tracy. "The Fourth of July . . ."

"And me flat on my back—of all days in the year! I got a real bad feeling about tomorrow. I don't doubt a minute that Reub Springer and that crowd he runs with are going to be on the prod, looking to get even with somebody for what happened this afternoon. And there'll be nobody to keep them in line!"

"How about Luft? Won't he put a curb on his man, when he hears the shape you're in—and finds out that it happened at the JL?"

"No." The marshal was wearily emphatic. "Luft won't raise a hand. He likes the idea of the JL being thought a tough outfit; and anyway, he doesn't give much of a damn what happens to us, here in Mitchell. You heard the way he was talking—he figures he's bigger than the town, and he may even be right. He knows we depend on the trade he gives us and that we'd have a hard time doing without it!"

Bannon frowned. "You're getting around to something, Marshal. What is it?"

"I need help," the hurt man told him. "I need somebody to take over for me. Someone who's shown he ain't afraid of Reub Springer—and someone John Luft ain't in a position to hurt. That lets out anybody in town that I can think of, except one—and I'm looking at him!"

The sharp blue stare rested on the man who stood by the bed, battered Stetson in hand. When Ed Bannon absorbed his meaning and hesitated over an answer, Sam Prentiss forged ahead. "I admired the way you handled yourself at the JL, the way you crowded Reub Springer and kept him off balance. I admit I don't know anything more about you than that; still, I know I'd feel a lot easier laying here tomorrow, if somebody like you was on the job in my place. Just how long I'm going to be laid up, I don't know and neither does the doc—though if he thinks he can keep me here longer than a couple weeks, he's bad mistaken. But anyhow, if you could use a temporary deputy's pay, there's at least a couple weeks' work in it. Just say the word, and I'll fix it up with the town commissioners. How about it, Bannon?"

Ed Bannon had no answer, for a moment, to this request made of a virtual stranger. Finally he said, "You overestimate me. All the same I'd like to say yes, if I could. If you hadn't got in the way of a bullet meant for me, you wouldn't be in this shape now—and so I was at least partly responsible."

"Frankly, that's occurred to me," the lawman said bluntly. "But I guess you're turning me down?"

"There just ain't any choice. I've got to be riding. I've already lost a whole day on this town of yours—a day I couldn't spare."

The blue eyes studied him. Suddenly the scarred and pallid cheeks stiffened and Sam Prentiss exclaimed, "Somebody's after you—that's it, ain't it? Oh, I've had a feeling about you, from the start . . . It's the law, I suppose?" Then he made a grimace and, not waiting for an answer, corrected himself, "Oh, hell! What difference would *that* have to make—if I can just get you to stay a little longer . . ."

But Ed Bannon shook his head. "Sorry," he told the lawman. "I'm afraid you can't." And to end the discussion, he turned and abruptly left.

Chapter 6

Still oddly troubled by that scene with Sam Prentiss,
rehearsing what was said and wondering if he could
have made his refusal less blunt and uncompromis-
ing, Bannon saw Kit Tracy hurrying toward him
with a man he guessed could only be her grandfather. Kit looked different. She had changed out of
her flounced Sunday dress into a long, dark skirt
and a comfortable-looking blouse that she wore
with the throat unbuttoned and the sleeves rolled
up on her strong brown arms. Her hair was caught
up under the brim of a flat-crowned, black straw hat.

"Mr. Bannon!" she was exclaiming as he came
down off the doctor's porch to meet them. "Howie
told us you were back and that you had the black
with you. He said you needed the doctor—for Sam
Prentiss!"

"I'm afraid that's right," Bannon said. "He was
hurt, out at the JL."

"Hurt bad?" she exclaimed and interrupted herself. "Oh—this is my grandpa. You can see, he got
home finally."

Orin Tracy, with his snow-white hair and beard
and stiffly erect figure, gave the impression of an old
man's fragility, but his eyes were unfaded and there
was a firm pressure in the hand that clasped Bannon's briefly. "So you're the stranger that's been

looking after my stock," he said in a voice that held a surprising bass rumble. "I'm obliged to you. Still, I just can't imagine John Luft making trouble for the law."

"It wasn't Luft," Bannon said. "He pretty much stayed out of it. But Reub Springer had been drinking, and he purely didn't want to give up the black. He and I had a little argument; he tried to settle it with a gun."

"*You* weren't hurt?" Kit said anxiously.

"No. There was only one shot—and Sam Prentiss happened to get in the way. Springer quieted down pretty quick, after that."

"And—Sam?"

"He took kind of a mean one. Though it could have been worse, according to your Doctor Ashby."

Bannon knew from the girl's expression that she wasn't satisfied with his too-brief account of the affair at the JL; but she let it go, frowning at him while her teeth worried her lower lip. Orin Tracy, for his part, said gruffly, "I mean to find out about Sam for myself." And he started for the steps.

The doctor had come out onto the porch. He lifted a warning hand, with a shake of the head as he told the old man, "Nothing doing! Sam Prentiss has got to rest. I won't have him disturbed."

"Nobody's disturbing him," Orin Tracy said flatly. "I only want a look." And he tramped past the doctor, pulled the screen door wide, and let himself into the house. Ashby looked at the old man's granddaughter, gave a shrug and a helpless shake of the head. He followed Orin Tracy inside, and Bannon and the girl were left alone.

"At least your grandfather knows what he wants," Ed Bannon suggested, with a smile.

"Yes, indeed!" she answered. "The only person in all his life who's ever been able to make him pull in his head has been my grandmother."

Ed Bannon thought of that tiny woman with the white hair and the brown eyes that were so much like Kit's, and the thought of her enforcing her will on someone as hard-nosed as Orin Tracy made him smile. Meanwhile the girl was continuing, earnestly, "Grandpa didn't say much about it, but I know he's grateful to you for returning the black. *I* think we owe you something. Reub Springer is completely unpredictable. Why, he might have killed you!"

"But he didn't," Bannon pointed out. "And that's all over and done, now . . ." So, it seemed, was the conversation. An awkward silence fell. Bannon looked at the rope-scarred hand that held his hat. He drew a breath. "Well! You and I seem to keep saying 'goodbye,' don't we? And now the time's come again."

"You *are* having a time getting out of this town," she agreed, with a smile. "Maybe, this once, you can make it stick."

Bannon looked at his dun horse, standing patiently on grounded reins. There, too, was the roan that Sam Prentiss had ridden to the JL. Indicating it, he said, "I forgot all about the marshal's horse. What do you suppose I should do with it?"

"Sam has a shed next to the jail," the girl said, "but now that he's laid up, there won't be anyone to look after it. I'd better just take it on down to the livery."

"Then perhaps I can travel that far with you . . ."

So the leave-taking had been postponed once more, for a last few minutes. For some reason, as they walked away from the doctor's place leading the animals, Ed Bannon felt a curious sense of loss.

There all at once seemed nothing to say. A silence fell upon them—it was Kit who broke it, suggesting, "With this late a start, I don't suppose you're going to get awfully far tonight."

"At least I can make a start—which is more than I've managed so far today. There's some daylight left; I can get a few hours in . . ." And then the silence seemed to claim them both.

Much of the canyon lay in shadow now, though the bare slope beyond the creek was still bathed in sunlight. They entered the street and turned down it toward the barn and corral, on the creek bank just this side of the shallow crossing.

At the foot of Nelson Street, three men leaned against a saloon hitching rail. They seemed involved in inconsequential talk, one of them hacking idly at the pole with the blade of a clasp knife. But in another moment it became clear they were doing something other than killing time there, for as Bannon and the girl approached a head turned, the man with the knife closed it and dropped it into a pocket, and as though by agreement all three moved away from the rail. With a few steps they were out into the street, pivoting and spreading a little apart, and then there could be no doubt that they had been waiting there on purpose.

Bannon glanced at Kit and surprised a look of alarm on her. He said gruffly, "You know them?"

"I've heard the skinny one in the middle called Nick Garvey. They're drinking cronies of Reub Springer's."

"Do they work for Luft?"

"I doubt that they work at all, except enough to keep Sam Prentiss from running them in for vagrancy. Reub helps keep them in likker."

Bannon thought that over as he and Kit moved ahead, unhurriedly, leading the horses. He rather imagined he had seen all three of the men that morning, in the crowd that gathered around the string of Cap Flynn's mustangs. He was certain at least of the one named Nick Garvey—a narrow-shouldered, stringy fellow in run-over boots and clothes that didn't look too clean, his bony jaws framed by the horns of a drooping handlebar moustache: Bannon had seen him a second time at the JL, with Springer, watching as Reub's baiting of the stranger ended in disaster. Plainly he'd brought the news to town to share with the rest of Springer's friends. Now Bannon saw him step away from the others and move forward a pace, with the clear intent of intercepting the stranger should he try to pass by.

So there was going to be no way around this, and grimly Ed Bannon accepted it. "Hang onto this for me," he told Kit and pressed one of his dun's split reins into the girl's hand. "And stay here."

"What are you going to do?" she exclaimed anxiously.

"That's sort of up to them." And leaving her with the horses, he veered his course directly toward the rawboned figure she had called Garvey.

Taken by surprise, the man stiffened and actually retreated a half step, but after that he held his ground; a wary expression came into his eyes. Bannon halted a couple of yards away—even from there he could smell the booze. He said coldly, "Well?"

Garvey didn't answer at once. He looked around nervously, as though making certain his friends were still there to back him up. Like Bannon, he wore a gun and holster, but only one of his companions appeared to have a weapon, shoved behind his pants belt. The unhurried run of Bridge Creek through its channel nearby seemed very loud, suddenly, in the town's Sunday stillness.

Ed Bannon was starting to lose patience. "Did you want to see me?"

The thin man's shoulders lifted as he drew a breath. He said, "No, but I sure as hell know somebody who does!"

"Reub Springer? I'd have thought he'd seen enough of me by this time."

Garvey replied to that with an obscenity. He said harshly, "Don't flatter yourself! All Reub wants is a chance to lay hands on you! If Luft hadn't stopped him, he'd have gone after you and settled things when you rode off with the black this afternoon. Right now he thinks you're on your way to Prineville—he's really gonna be happy when we tell him he ain't missed his chance at you after all!"

"I hate to disappoint you," Bannon retorted coldly. "The marshal getting hurt made a little hitch in my getting started for Prineville when I planned; but my plans ain't changed at all. I'm certainly not going to stay around this place forever, just to satisfy Reub Springer!"

"No?" Garvey was beginning to build his confidence. "Well, you see how it is. Us three are Reub's friends. As a favor I think we'll just have to see to it you *do* stay around. You ain't going nowhere!"

"I think you're mistaken."

"No I ain't!" And the man's bony hand came up and it was holding the gun from his holster.

Bannon stiffened, and he heard a startled cry from Kit Tracy. At the same time, as though belatedly picking up a cue, the other man who carried a pistol fumbled and got it out from behind his belt. All at once Ed Bannon found himself facing two drawn weapons. The fact that they were being held by men who were probably more than half drunk didn't make the situation any pleasanter. Careful to make no sudden or startling move, he said, with a throat suddenly gone dry, "You'd better be sure you know what you're doing!"

Nick Garvey was swaggering now, thoroughly pleased with himself. "You ain't got things all your own way this time, Bannon. And according to what we hear, you can't look for no help from the marshal, either."

Or from anyone else, he might as well have added. Main Street was nearly deserted, this summer Sunday evening. At the entrance of Weiker's Emporium, close by, Bannon saw a young man in his shirt sleeves, with a coat slung over his arm, who had let himself out of the store and was just in the act of locking the glass-paned double doors behind him. Whoever he was—a clerk, probably—he was staring over his shoulder now at the men in the street, and his face looked white and alarmed in the shadow of the porch roof. He stood rooted there, as though frozen.

Most appalling of all, Bannon was aware of Kit Tracy standing almost directly behind him. He remembered what a wild bullet had done to Sam Prentiss, and thought of the girl being exposed to a similar danger was like a weight that settled heavily into place inside him. He could see then what he was going to have to do.

He drew a breath and said, in a tone as calmly persuasive as he could make it, "Now, you men know you aren't going to use those things. It's no favor, holding me for Reub Springer, if you go and shoot me yourselves—he'll be pretty much put out over it!"

He let them think about that, saw it take some of the edge off their cockiness. Pressing, he went on in the same reasonable tone: "And you surely don't think I'd stand a chance taking on the lot of you. Why don't you put the guns away?" He spread both his hands, palms upward, to show them empty. "Personally I think we better talk this over," he told Garvey. "What do *you* think?"

Garvey didn't seem to know—having it put to him like that appeared to fuddle him. He scowled fiercely, jaw working beneath the straggling horns of his moustache. When Ed Bannon took a step toward him, his head jerked and he raised the barrel of the gun indecisively. Bannon came another step; still the man hesitated. And then a single quick stride closed the remaining distance and the edge of Bannon's left hand, chopping down, caught the gun and knocked it out of line while his other fist swung hard.

His knuckles landed solidly on the hinge of a bony jaw. Whiskey breath gusted out of Garvey and he went down in a loose pile. And now Ed Bannon, standing over him, had his own revolver out and pointed at Reub Springer's friends. To the one who held a gun he said sharply, "Drop that! Or use it—I don't particularly care right now!"

Bug-eyed and thoroughly shaken, the man had no real choice. He didn't drop the gun, but hastily laid it on the ground and then straightened with his hands beside his ears. The third man, not being armed, presented no problem. Garvey was propped on an elbow, rubbing his sore jaw and eying his own weapon which had fallen just out of reach. But he made no attempt to try for it, and when Bannon said sharply, "Get up!" he obeyed meekly enough.

It had all happened in a matter of seconds—it was doubtful whether anyone had even noticed, except for Kit Tracy and the young fellow watching from the porch at Weiker's. But knowing how the thing could have turned out all too easily had made this a moment of decision for Ed Bannon.

The danger to Kit hardened his face and his voice as he told the three under his gun: "I want you to listen to me! With Sam Prentiss laid up, you seem to think you'll have things around here to suit yourselves—that it's going to be the old days all over again, when Mitchell was a wide-open town and the people who lived here had to take their chances. Well, you can think again! Sam asked me a little while ago if I'd fill in as temporary marshal until he got back on his feet; I turned him down. But you three have changed my mind for me. I see now that somebody's got to do his job—and since I'm part of the reason he can't do it for himself, I guess it's up to me!

"Pass this word along," he instructed them. "Tomorrow being a holiday doesn't mean it's a field day for the likes of you. The first man who makes trouble or disturbs the peace here in Mitchell—if it's so much as spitting on the sidewalk—he goes to jail. I won't fool with him! I don't care who he is—or, for that matter, who he works for. Is that understood?"

He threw his challenge at the trio and got no answer. But he thought they had the message, and he concluded, briefly, "Think about it . . . I'm holding your guns for the time being. Now, move along!"

They went—Garvey and the other one left their

weapons lying in the dirt—and Bannon watched them move off down the street. His nerves were still tight, and when Kit came up beside him and laid a hand on his arm the muscle jumped involuntarily. She said something he scarcely heard.

All this long day, he thought with a kind of sour irony, he had been like a man trying vainly to escape his destiny. From the moment he reached this town, it was as though one event after another had been conspiring to hold him, to draw him back and hem him in—until, now, he stood committed out of his own mouth. His options were closed. Henceforth he had no choice but to go with the tide and hope for the best.

The jail, set off by itself on Nelson Street at some distance up the hill from Main, was a one-story, whitewashed structure. Having put his own horse and the marshal's in the shed at the rear, Bannon tried the jail door and was not too surprised to find it unlocked. The layout consisted of one large room that had a single cell, a cage with a barred door, built into one rear corner. There was a desk and a few chairs, a stove, a cot with rumpled blankets, a gun rack under lock and chain which held a rifle and a shotgun. That was about the extent of the furnishings.

Ed Bannon walked in, leaving the door open, and dropped his saddlebags in a corner behind the desk. He was none too sure of protocol. He hadn't been able to talk to Sam Prentiss again—the marshal was asleep and Doc Ashby had refused to disturb him. But he saw no reason to believe Prentiss' job offer wasn't still good, and he dropped into the chair behind the desk while he pondered his next move.

A man appeared in the open doorway.

He was a stranger to Bannon, but he came in as though he had important business. Sharp black eyes in a jowly, clean-shaven face probed at Bannon and prompted him to suggest, "If you're looking for Prentiss—"

The man interrupted. "I know all about Sam Prentiss—I was just now trying to see him, but the doc wouldn't let me. I'm Jess Weiker." He added, for emphasis, "*Mayor* Weiker . . ."

"Very glad to know you. The name's Ed Bannon." He indicated a chair across the desk from him. "Have a seat. I imagine we have things to talk about."

Weiker hesitated and then accepted, letting himself onto the edge of the chair as though he only perched there momentarily. He had the look of a successful small-town merchant, a man of nervous movements and small importances; a man in his mid-forties, soft of body, with a head held stiffly erect as though the tight celluloid collar served it as a brace. The black eyes stared at the other man and Weiker said crisply, "So you're Bannon. I hear you claim that Sam Prentiss has asked you to fill in for him."

"News gets around," Bannon said. "I do claim that. You can check it with Prentiss when the doctor will let him have visitors."

"Don't worry—I mean to. The thing is," Weiker continued, "Sam Prentiss has no authority to make such an appointment. Not without approval from the mayor, and the town council."

"I see." Without hesitation Bannon pushed back his chair. "It's all right with me. I never wanted the job—it was all your marshal's idea. I turned him down once. Just as well I didn't have a chance to tell him I'd changed my mind." He got to his feet and was taking his hat from the peg where he'd hung it before the other man found his voice.

"Now, wait!" Jess Weiker had been taken by surprise. He flushed and said, "I didn't mean we couldn't talk this over! Sam must have had his reasons. Please—come back and sit down."

That must have been hard for him, and Ed Bannon relented. With a shrug he put his hat back on the peg and returned to his seat. But having done that, he waited, leaving it for the other man to put their conversation back on the track.

"The only trouble," the mayor said, a good deal less officiously now, "is that no one appears to know anything about you—neither Ashby, nor Orin Tracy, or anyone else I've talked to. On the other hand, I did have report of what happened down on the street not over an hour ago—a little trouble, I understand, with some of that saloon crowd. I heard you handled it very well. I must admit, I liked the sound of that."

"Thanks," Ed Bannon said briefly.

"I realize, of course," Weiker continued, "the party I heard this from might have been exaggerating. Young Bert Maroon is a clerk at my store, who'd gone down to fetch something he left when he closed up yesterday evening and happened to see this affair. I'm afraid he's sort of impressionable. Tends to hero worship."

Bannon remembered him, of course—staring, motionless, from the doorway of Weiker's Emporium. He nodded. "Maroon could have built it up some. There was a man named Garvey who wanted some trouble, only he wanted to talk about it. Once they make the mistake of talking, they're generally not too hard to manage."

Jess Weiker drummed his fingers on the desk top, as he measured the other man from beneath lowered brows. Abruptly, then, he slapped the desk and came to his feet. He was still businesslike but his manner had changed since he came bustling into the jail. He said, "All right, Bannon. I wanted a look at you, to size you up for myself. I'm satisfied.

"One thing certain—with a holiday tomorrow, this town can't very well afford to be without *some* kind of law enforcement. I'm sure the rest of the council will agree. Personally I don't know anyone else that would be willing, or qualified, to step into the job at a moment's notice. So if Sam thinks you can handle it, I'm ready to cooperate any way I can."

"That sounds fair," Bannon said. "I figure to do the same." Weiker offered a hand and Bannon reached across the desk and shook with him. A moment later the mayor was gone.

He left Ed Bannon with considerable to think about. It had never promised to be easy, stepping into this situation—cold—and managing it in a way to suit Sam Prentiss. What he hadn't really given much thought to was the politics of the thing. There were more people than Sam that he'd have to please, more even than the mayor and the other town officials. Every resident and every visitor to Mitchell would be watching him tomorrow, to see how he performed. There was probably no way to satisfy them all.

But meanwhile he might as well make himself comfortable, and be thinking about something to eat. When Kit had learned his decision she'd immediately invited him to supper with her family but, having imposed on the Tracys once already today, he'd declined. If truth were told, after that solid noon meal, he wasn't sure he could handle more of such hospitality. He was accustomed to trail rations and not to the generous fare these people of Mitchell, with their teeming gardens, apparently accepted as normal. On a shelf he found a bag of Arbuckle's, a coffee mill, and part of a box of crackers. That should do fine.

As he set about his preparations, using the graniteware coffeepot on the stove and building a fire with wood from the kindling box, he had time for some long thoughts. It was unsettling enough to find himself virtually trapped in a town he'd never even known existed before hearing Cap Flynn mention it yesterday. What made it more disturbing was the girl, Kit Tracy.

There was no way to deny the strong appeal she had for him, nor the real concern she'd shown during his brush with Nick Garvey and those other two, down there on the street. Afterward, when it was all over, her pleasure at learning he meant to stay awhile here in Mitchell couldn't have been more obvious. But he shook his head over the steaming cup he held between his palms. Kit was a warm person, with a liking for people, and in this isolated spot it wasn't often she would be apt to see a new face. Ed Bannon had brought excitement and a hint of danger she likely found intriguing. It was nothing more than that.

And he had to remember there were good reasons why he had no business thinking seriously of any woman, just now.

He finished his sketchy meal, rinsed out the china cup in water from the bucket, put things away. As he was doing so, the sound of a bell tolling reached him in the quiet and he paused to listen. That would mean Sunday evening church service, he thought, and wondered if the Tracys would be there. With his mind so full of Kit it would be nice to have another look at her, but he had already admitted during dinner that he wasn't much of a churchgoer. He wouldn't want anyone to get an idea he was chasing after her.

Instead, he opted for another look at the upper town in what was left of daylight.

Dusk had already settled in the canyon, but when he climbed the steps he found a glow of sunset still lay across Piety Hill. People were still entering the church, though by now its bell had fallen silent. Ed Bannon strolled along the lanes of the village, observing that Kit had surely been right when she told him everyone here prided himself on his garden. Nearly every available level bit of ground had been broken and given over to cultivation, and he saw people busily pruning roses or weeding vegetable patches. He stopped a time or two to introduce himself and chat briefly. Although surprised to see a stranger in town, the ones he spoke to seemed glad to talk to him and proudly show him the results of their labor and of this fruitful place. Nearly all repeated what Sam Prentiss had told him—there was no place they would rather live.

Despite its remoteness and isolation, Bannon was beginning to sense that for those who liked its easy pace of life, this village could be a source of real contentment. As he listened to the shouts of children playing in the dusk and the occasional popping of a firecracker as someone started tomorrow's celebrating ahead of time, he stopped to pick a handful of ripe cherries from a tree branch overhanging the pathway. Eating them, he went down off the bench and entered Main Street, in the canyon by the creek.

This section might have been part of an entirely different town. There seemed to be no Sunday closure for the saloons; three were open and doing business with the particular gusto of the night before a holiday. Bannon looked into each as he went past but saw nothing untoward. And thus he came to the doctor's cottage, to inquire after Sam Prentiss' condition.

"Why don't you step in and see for yourself?" Ashby suggested.

"I can talk to him?"

For answer he was ushered in and motioned toward the sick room. Sam Prentiss was propped up with pillows at his back; by the lamp on the table nearby, his color looked a good deal better than it had—rest and the care he was getting seemed to be serving him well already. Before Bannon could ask a question, the marshal cut him off, blurting a comment of his own. "Well! I been hearing about you, mister—from Jess Weiker, chiefly. Frankly I'm surprised. I thought your mind was set on leaving. I never thought to see you change it. In fact, I never thought to see you again."

"Me either," Ed Bannon told him. "But it looks like something happened."

"Something named Nick Garvey?" And at the other's nod: "Just what was the nature of that? Jess Weiker told me what he'd heard, but I'd like to get it from you. Pull up a chair!"

But Bannon remained standing, hat in hand, while he told as much of the incident as he thought the marshal needed to know. He said, in concluding: "It didn't really amount to anything; but it showed me you were right! With people like that around, there could be trouble—tomorrow, or later—and someone had to be ready to stop it. If I was the one you wanted, it looked like I couldn't do less than try."

Sam Prentiss rubbed a palm across stubbled cheeks. "I dunno, Bannon," he said finally. "We both know you had your reasons for turning me down when I asked you. Stands to reason things ain't changed any. Then, how can you—?"

Bannon interrupted. "Let that be my concern," he said bluntly, as he turned to go. "Don't worry about it . . ." At the door he paused. "This much I'll tell you, Sam. The trouble I'm trying to avoid is a personal matter—nothing to do with the law, to my knowledge anyway. So you see, you guessed wrong on that point."

The blue eyes studied him. The marshal nodded his head against the pillows. "If you say so, I'll believe you. Incidentally, I've got Jess Weiker's promise to back you with any help you need from the council."

"He told me he'd put in a word with them. Right now, the most help *you* can do me is to hurry up and mend, so I can turn this job back to you!"

"I'm working on it," Sam Prentiss said.

Chapter 7

The Fourth was going to be very much like the day before—full of bright sun and cool cloud shadow and enough light breeze to keep the July heat from settling. A rooster somewhere on Piety Hill crowed the morning in, and others answered it, and almost immediately a banging of firecrackers began as the town kids, their breakfasts bolted, got down to this day's serious business.

At the marshal's office, Ed Bannon had been awake before the roosters. He made up his bunk and then proceeded to dress and shave with particular care. He had no illusions about today. He was going to be on exhibition, a target of curious stares and speculation; the impression the people of this town got of him would be a reflection on Sam Prentiss, who had chosen him.

He heated up the coffeepot and was standing in the open door, cup in hand, when the mayor came bustling by on his way down the hill to Main Street. There was a young girl with him, and he introduced her. "This is my daughter Adeline."

Bannon remembered mention of an Addie Weiker who was Kit's best friend. She struck him as one of those pretty girls who look like a hundred other pretty girls. He greeted her politely, but her father had no time for conversation.

Weiker was already perspiring under the day's responsibilities. He had a bunch of papers in his hand and he gave one to Bannon, saying, "Here's a copy of the schedule. I thought you'd find it useful to know what's happening, and when."

Bannon looked it over. The program appeared fairly elaborate—a morning parade, a baseball game, and in the afternoon a barbecue and speeches and dancing . . . "Who plays in the ball game?" he wanted to know.

"We have us a team," the mayor assured him. "And the ranch crews from out of town generally manage to put one together." Weiker's suspicions toward the acting marshal seemed considerably eased this morning, probably from his having talked with Sam Prentiss. He told Bannon, "Everything's set, and the council's in agreement. If you look in the desk, I think you might find a leftover deputy marshal's badge. I'd like you to pin it on, let people know who you are."

"All right."

The Weikers left, Addie with a last coquettish glance that made Ed Bannon wish he knew what Kit Tracy might have said about him. He found the badge in the clutter at the back of a drawer. *A first time for everything*, he thought wryly, as he polished the tarnished bit of metal on his coat sleeve as best he could and pinned it to his shirt. He took a moment to check on the horses in the shed behind the office. Afterward he put on his hat and stepped out into Nelson Street, carefully closing the door behind him.

The day was getting noisier. Somebody had rigged up a carbide cannon and its sporadic booming sent echoes through the canyon, cutting across the smaller racket of firecrackers. By now, too, there was activity down on Main Street—he heard an occasional booming of a big drum, the squawk of a comet running flourishes. As people came streaming down off the bench, there were curious stares for the stranger standing before the jail door. Bannon tipped his hat politely a time or two but received not so much as a nod. *They're suspicious,* he thought. The hell with them . . .

When he reached the foot of the hill he saw that Main Street was filling up. Rigs and saddle horses lined the hitching rails or filled the vacant lots. The bright dresses and parasols of the women wove strands of color into the drab texture of male garb. Men off the range, and others who could have come from mine workings back in the hills, had gathered on saloon porches or clogged the flow of traffic on the sidewalks to catch up on their talk. A busy hubbub of voices rolled along the street. Bannon saw a gleam of sunlight caught in the bell of a tuba, heard the squeals and the stir of horses as someone let off a string of firecrackers under the heels of a hitching-rail lineup.

Attentive and alert, aware of the curious looks he got, he moved through the crowd to the livery, where he wanted to check on the black stud. The black, in a pen by himself, looked nervous at the odd and disruptive sounds going on around him. He worried the dirt of the corral with his hooves and eyed Bannon dubiously. It was almost as though he couldn't be quite sure now whether this man he had fought with was really an enemy or, perhaps, someone who understood and sympathized. Bannon told him, "Take it easy, boy."

A moment later he found Howie Whipple leading

a customer's horse into a stall while a couple of others waited to be unsaddled. Howie was sweating and busy; he threw Bannon a rueful look and said, "It's a holiday—but I'm working!"

"Same with me," Bannon commented.

He followed the hostler back into the shadows of the barn to watch as Howie shoved the animal into a stall. Howie had seen the badge on the other man's shirtfront. He pointed a finger at it. "So you tooken Sam Prentiss's job."

"Just until he's on his feet again." Bannon changed the subject: "A lot of outsiders in town today. Even so, I imagine you know a lot of them."

"I know the regulars, from the ranches and so on. But there's bound to be faces I never seen before. Working where I do, though, I generally get a look at them all."

"How's your memory for faces?"

Howie Whipple considered. "Good as most, I guess. Though I remember horses better."

"Happens there's someone I'm keeping an eye out for." Bannon repeated the description he had given Cap Flynn a couple of days before: "He's a well-set-up fellow, probably clean-shaven; fair-haired with a touch of red in it. You'll notice an old scar, here on his right cheek . . ."

Howie Whipple stored the picture away in his mind somewhere. He suggested doubtfully, "If he shows, you want I should tell him you're looking for him?"

"Don't tell him anything. Just be sure you tell *me*."

That got him a sharp look. But the hostler evidently knew when he wasn't supposed to ask questions, whatever his curiosity might be. "Sure thing, Mr. Bannon," he said.

Ed Bannon started back up the street, glimpses of Bridge Creek showing between the scattered buildings, its waters sparkling beyond a fringe of willows and creek-bank scrub. He tested the sounds that came to him from the open doors of the town's saloons; he knew it was possible that way to judge the temper of the crowd within. As yet he had seen none of John Luft's crew, which could have been a signal to watch out for trouble.

Meanwhile he found himself expecting to catch a glimpse of Kit Tracy. A couple of times he was sure that he had and felt an unexpected lift of pleasure, but when she turned her head he saw it was another girl. The second time this happened he caught himself up, with a grimace and the thought, *Don't be a fool! Keep your mind on the job . . .*

Without fanfare, the band instruments suddenly struck up a number. The Fourth of July parade was under way.

It came winding down the street from somewhere near the head of it, up where the canyon road twisted into view past a big flour mill. It consisted of exactly three floats—plain flatbed wagons that someone must have spent hours decorating with colored crepe paper. Even the wheels had been festooned, and each two-horse team had tassels fastened to its harness. The band rode on the first wagon—a tuba, bass drum, cornet, fiddle, and banjo; Ed Bannon decided they were trying to render "There'll Be a Hot Time in the Old Town Tonight." They lumbered down Main between two lines of cheering and hat-waving bystanders, and behind them came the second wagon carrying a large woman dressed as the Statue of Liberty, with a cardboard torch and crown.

Bannon wondered who the woman might be, to

have the honor; she looked a bit like Addie Weiker—
she could be the mayor's wife, but if so, she must
have several pounds on her husband. The third and
final wagon bore a tableau of Washington crossing
the Delaware in a cotton wig and a homemade cos-
tume, standing in a rowboat with two men at the
oars. Washington was having trouble keeping his
three-cornered hat in place and maintaining his balance and his dignity amid the teasing of his friends
along the sidelines.

Bannon had been watching the crowd more than
the parade itself, and when he noted a couple of
half-grown boys with their heads together he knew
he had found what he was looking for. He moved toward them behind the line of spectators, without
hurry. One had a good-sized firecracker and the other
a piece of glowing punk. Both were so intent on light-
ing up that they failed to see Ed Bannon until he
loomed over them and they heard him say calmly, "I
don't think I'd do that, boys."

They looked up, startled at sight of the badge and
the face above it. Their intent, of throwing their firecracker under the horses and disrupting the historic
Delaware crossing and probably the whole parade,
could not have been plainer, but they gave it up
quickly enough and ducked off into the crowd. The
wagons rolled ponderously on down to splash across
the creek and there probably take a turnabout and
return to the starting place. The notes of the musical
instruments pattered thin echoes off building fronts
and canyon walls. There was a spattering of ap-
plause as the crowd broke and the street filled again.

It was in that moment Bannon saw Kit Tracy, on
the opposite walk.

She was with her friend Addie and another girl.

He didn't know whether they had noticed him or not, but they gave no sign of it and he dropped the hand he had half lifted. But he stood for a long moment looking after them, until he lost sight of Kit Tracy in the shifting crowd.

There had been no more than the brief glimpse of the girl laughing and chatting with her friends, tossing her head back in a way that he had noticed before. But it took only that to confirm, definitely, a thing that he had been trying not to admit.

God damn it! he thought, angry with himself. *You've done it! I think you've gone and lost your head over that girl! Now why did you have to do that?*

But when she left his sight she took some of the brightness out of the day.

Sam Prentiss said, "How'd you like the parade?"

Bannon caught the dry amusement and answered in the same tone. "I admit I've seen better."

"Likely enough. Sounded from here like the music was up to its usual. Did Mamie Weiker do her Statue of Liberty again?"

"She did. I'm sorry you had to miss it."

"There'll always be next year. I'll try to wait." Prentiss shifted position slightly against the pillows at his back and Bannon saw him wince. The lawman's color was better this morning; he was getting good care and it looked like simply a matter of time. But a bullet hole like that one didn't heal overnight, and there was no way you could hurry it.

The holiday noise and the crack of exploding fireworks came in through the window on a warm noontime stir of air. Having answered Bannon's questions, the marshal had a question of his own. "Luft and his crowd showed up?"

"Not that I've noticed," Bannon said.

"You'd have noticed! They always come in a bunch, and they don't make a secret of it. Even if John Luft sneers at our town, he damn well wants us to know when he's around." The marshal added, "But if everything's peaceful so far, well and good; any trouble will come later. I'd suggest you keep an eye on Chipman's place. The tough element makes it their headquarters."

"That kind of a place, is it?"

"Not actually," the marshal said. "Wilcey Chipman's not a bad fellow. He stocks the best whiskey in town, and that's one reason why Reub Springer and his friends favor it. Truth is, Chipman just doesn't know how to handle that crowd. They got him buffaloed, and he knows it."

Bannon took his hat from the bed where he had laid it. "All right. I'll have a look . . ."

Chipman's, near the head of the canyon street, was the largest saloon in Mitchell and, to judge by the flow of traffic across the porch and through the hooked-back doors, one of the most popular. Ed Bannon could see why. Wilcey Chipman had spent money to make it attractive. Most saloons were cramped and dingy places, with dark walls and pressed-tin ceilings. Here, by contrast, was room to move around and actually enough windows to let in light and air. The cherry-wood bar was fancy enough to rival some he'd seen in bigger towns than this. The chairs at the gaming tables had comfortable-looking leather seats. And he remembered what Prentiss had told him, about Chipman stocking the best bar goods.

Well, that was how it went sometimes—a businessman went to extra expense and made a special effort to give his place better class than some of his competitors, with the result that the wrong people were attracted and ended up by taking over.

Ed Bannon worked through the mill of noisy customers, scanning faces, taking the temper of the place. So it was that he reached an area at the back of the room where a couple of pool tables stood in a kind of alcove; and here he suddenly came face to face with Nick Garvey. Leaning over the green-topped table, cue in hand, Garvey saw him and quickly straightened. "Bannon!" he sang out, and came around the table while other players faded back out of the way. As he did, an eddy of stillness, built by his carrying voice, began to spread through that section of the room. "Just where the hell is my gun?"

"At the jail, of course," Ed Bannon told him. "Where'd you think?"

"I want it."

"No."

The room seemed to be concentrated on them now, as they stood confronted—the bony, stoop-shouldered Garvey and the solid Ed Bannon with his black moustache making a bold slash across his sunbrowned face. Garvey's hands worked on the cue, his mouth, framed by the horns of a down-sweeping moustache, showing an angry twist. He indicated the men around them as he said, "All these other guys have got their guns. Why do you keep mine?"

Actually, only a few of the crowd openly showed weapons—men who had worn them in off the range; the townspeople seemed to be unarmed. Not arguing the point, Bannon shrugged and said, "The difference is, these others know how to mind their business. You can have your gun back tomorrow."

Nick Garvey scowled. "I may not be here tomorrow."

"That would be good news," Bannon said dryly. "Any time you're ready to leave town, come by the jail and pick up your weapon. The same goes for the pair who were with you last evening. But remember—I'll see to it you *do* leave!"

Garvey showed his anger. His jaw pushed forward and his knuckles tightened on the cue. Aware of the damage the cue could do if used as a weapon, Bannon suggested, "You want to try something with that? Then go right ahead!"

It was a direct challenge that Garvey wasn't ready to take up. He swore, and he whipped around and rapped the pointed end of the cue at an ivory ball with such angry force that the ball jumped the far end of the table. Two men standing there yelled and split out of the way as it struck the wall between them. Nick Garvey flung down his cue on the felt top with a clatter, and he turned and elbowed his way toward the bar, passing Ed Bannon without another look—but close enough for Bannon to see the bunched muscles of his lean jaw and the faint beads of moisture shining there. The man, he realized suddenly, was at least a little frightened!

Bannon, for his part, had nothing but contempt for this Nick Garvey who only fancied himself tough, probably in emulation of Reub Springer whom he admired. Perhaps, Bannon thought, he'd let a little too much of that contempt show in the way he had used his tongue . . . Now, as someone spoke at his elbow, he looked about and saw a man whose expression showed disapproval of what he had just witnessed. This man said, looking at the badge, "Are you the new marshal?"

"Acting marshal. You're Chipman?"

The other nodded. He was a fairly large man of about fifty, grown soft with middle age. Graying brown hair had receded over a wide forehead and his jowls were turning pendulous. He wore the neckband of his striped shirt buttoned, without a tie or collar, and the bowl of a cold pipe was thrust into a pocket of his open waistcoat. As the talk began again around them he told Bannon, "The way you just handled Nick Garvey—that was kind of rough. I'm not sure Sam Prentiss—"

Bannon interrupted him. "Look! Sam's methods are his own; mine are mine. He has to live in this town—I don't. I'll only be here a few days, and I just haven't time to be patient with someone like Garvey."

"I see." Wilcey Chipman's tone didn't hold much conviction. "I *think* . . . I'm afraid I don't see the good of deliberately antagonizing a man like that."

"I'm trying to keep order. It's too bad if Nick Garvey thinks I'm stepping on his toes."

"But if he's provoked, he could do anything. Maybe even break up my establishment!"

Ed Bannon considered. This Chipman was probably a good businessman, though maybe not quite tough enough for the particular business he happened to be in. Operating a saloon took guts and a tough hide and the determination to take nothing off any drunk or other potential troublemaker; Bannon wasn't sure the man had all those qualities.

Seeing Chipman seemed genuinely troubled, Bannon relented enough to tell him, "I won't apologize for my methods, but I'll back them. If you have more trouble with Nick Garvey or any of those people—get word to me and I'll come and take care of it. You have my promise. All right?"

The saloon owner looked dubious, but he nodded. "All right."

"Good!" Bannon said. "I have to go now and look in on a baseball game."

The playing diamond was located on Piety Hill, occupying an open flat near the schoolhouse. Bannon saddled his horse and rode up there, not knowing when an emergency might require his presence in some other part of town in a hurry. The noise of the crowd guided him. They filled the bleachers along the base lines with a dazzle of white shirts and women's summer dresses and parasols, while the overflow milled about the edges of the field and risked interfering with the players. Bannon found a place to tie and walked over for a look at the way the game was going.

Passions seemed to be running high. He gathered that the team who wore the baseball caps were the Mitchell players; the ones who didn't were the visitors. The umpire behind the plate looked familiar, and when he turned his head to call a ball on the batter he proved to be Orin Tracy. This led Bannon to hunt for Kit and he located her with her friend Addie Weiker, seated at the near end of the third-base bleachers. She had already spotted him and was signaling to him, and he walked over there.

A young man in a baseball cap, who held a bat and was using it self-consciously to knock mud from nonexistent cleats, lounged against the end of the bleachers. Bannon recognized him instantly from having seen him on the porch of Weiker's store last evening, watching wide-eyed his encounter with Nick Garvey. When Bannon had greeted the two girls, Kit introduced him to the ballplayer: "And this is Bert Maroon. I think he's been looking forward to meeting you."

Young Maroon seemed enthusiastic and respectful as he stuck a store clerk's hand into Bannon's. "I sure have, Mr. Bannon," he exclaimed. "I saw how you handled those men last night. I thought one of them was going to start shooting, for sure. But you never took a thing off them—you were completely sure of yourself, every minute!"

"Maybe not every minute," Bannon said briefly; such open admiration made him uncomfortable. To sidetrack the boy he switched the subject. "How's the game?"

"They're only one run ahead of us. We'll catch up."

Just then the batter knocked an easy pop fly into the glove of a visiting outfielder, and amid cheers and groans the side was retired. Addie Weiker said, "Well, you've still got a chance to catch them, but I don't think you'll make it. This is the last inning."

Bert Maroon gave her a hurt look. As he tossed his bat aside and went trotting out to take his position in center field, Bannon thought, *There's a youngster trying to make an impression on his girl and not getting anywhere very fast.* The Weiker girl was either genuinely indifferent or giving a good performance. She twirled her parasol and posed with lifted chin, like a blasé young woman rather bored by this whole business of a small-town baseball game.

Kit Tracy, by contrast, was her usual enthusiastic self. "How do you like our Fourth of July?" she asked Bannon.

"I'll know better when I've seen more of it," he told her. "So far it hasn't given me any trouble to speak of, and I'll be glad to see it stay that way." He inquired after her grandmother, was told the old lady had been up since dawn, busy with preparations for the barbecue. Orin Tracy called a strike on the visiting team's batter, raising a cheer from the Mitchell supporters. Bannon observed, "Your grandfather seems to be enjoying himself. Do these cowboys ever make trouble over his calls?"

"Oh, no," she said. "Everybody knows he's fair— he wouldn't deliberately favor the home players. After all, he has to be impartial. He does business with all of them."

The game continued—it was a short one, limited to five innings so as not to interfere with the barbecue, and now in the final inning the visitors were being held to their one-run lead. Bannon excused himself to the girls and went off through the milling crowd, taking its temper.

A couple of men were arguing Orin Tracy's call of the last pitch. Bannon moved up in a break and said pleasantly, "You boys enjoying yourselves?"

"Who wants to know?" one retorted, turning on him.

Whether it was something in Ed Bannon's expression or manner that did it or perhaps the sight of the badge pinned to his shirtfront, the man broke off and dropped back a step, scowling.

Bannon looked from one to the other. He said coolly, "Let's not let ourselves get worked up about nothing. It would be a pity if I had to run you in. All right?" He let the weight of his stare rest on them, daring either of them to make an argument. "All right?" he said again, putting pressure on them both and was rewarded by a couple of grudging nods. He accepted that, said, "That's fine," and abruptly turned his back and moved away, leaving them silent behind him.

It had all been done so quietly that it drew hardly any attention amid the noisy hubbub around them; but before he moved out of earshot he heard someone saying, "You fellows know who that was, don't you?" He caught a mention of Nick Garvey, and as he was swallowed by the noisy crowd he had the bleak satisfaction of knowing that word of him was already in process of being spread through the town. Well, he supposed he could use the advertising.

The final inning dragged itself out. The two teams seemed about evenly matched, neither being very good. A base on balls and a fielding error by the home team put a couple of runners on, but one of these let himself get trapped between second and third base and was run down and tagged out. On the next pitch the batter let go with an easy pop fly and the side was retired, still a run ahead, and Mitchell now had its last chance to change the picture.

It was Bert Maroon who came up to bat, cheered by the hometown crowd. Perhaps they gave him the boost he needed, or, Bannon thought, it might have been Addie Weiker watching in the stands, or maybe a simple lucky fluke. In any event, on the second pitch he sent a drive straight at the buckaroo playing right field. The man caught it, bobbled it, and let it roll between his legs, and while the crowd yelled itself hoarse young Bert Maroon went into third base standing up. Bannon watched as Bert, flushed with excitement, checked the bleachers to make certain Addie Weiker had seen. She waved her parasol while Kit Tracy, beside her on the wooden bench, clapped her hands and shouted her approval.

But that, unfortunately, was the high point of the

game for him and for Mitchell. The next two batters both popped out on the first balls pitched to them, and Maroon was still standing on third, stranded there, when Orin Tracy called a third strike on the final batter at the plate and told him, "You're out! Now let's go have us some barbecue!"

The final score stood unchanged: Visitors, 2—Mitchell, 1.

Bannon made his way through the crowd to intercept Maroon as he approached the bleachers, wholly crestfallen now after his triumph of only minutes before. "That was too bad," Bannon said and meant it. "You just didn't get the breaks. But there's nothing to blame yourself for. You hit a good triple."

Addie Weiker, coming down off the bleachers with Kit Tracy, heard that and told the young man, "It was all your fault, Bert. You should have made it a home run—then you'd have tied the score and the game would have had to go to extra innings."

Young Maroon threw her a look of hurt and despair. He started to say something, but he was crushed. He shrugged heavily and turned away, giving a kick at a stone, and marched off with his head down and his hands shoved deep in his pockets, to join the crowd streaming toward the path leading down off Piety Hill. Bannon heard Kit tell her friend, sternly, "You're being mean, to tease him so!"

Addie passed that off, saying defensively, "He asks for it. Always such a show-off!"

"But he isn't!" the other girl protested. "He's a very nice boy. He only wants to try and make you notice him. You know he's in love with you, Addie!"

"Oh, pooh!"

Bannon, moving off to get his horse, found himself thinking of the differences in people—particularly, in pretty women. Too many, like Mayor Weiker's smug little minx of a daughter, were aware of their attractions and used them without mercy. On the other hand, there was Kit Tracy, who had twice Addie Weiker's looks yet appeared completely unconscious of them. She hardly seemed to belong to the same species. He was considering the difference as he mounted and turned his horse into the wagon road that looped down off the bench, to join Nelson Street and so descend to the canyon floor.

The center of activity had shifted now to a flat stretch along the creek bank that appeared to serve Mitchell for a picnic ground. He could see horses and rigs tied up and people moving around; the hazy smoke and tempting aroma of the barbecue drifting along the canyon breeze were invitation enough. Before heading in that direction Ed Bannon took another unhurried swing along the street. The town's population looked almost to have doubled since morning, but on the whole, things seemed orderly. Bannon completed his tour and was turning toward the picnic ground when a familiar voice hailed him.

He reined in, surprised, as Cap Flynn made toward him through the street traffic.

The mustanger was aboard a tough-looking animal that was as short on beauty as its rider. One of Flynn's boots was missing, the hurt leg wrapped bulkily in rags. Bannon waited for the man to pull abreast of him, and he said, "I wasn't expecting to see *you* here. You're supposed to be laid up."

Narrow shoulders lifted in a shrug. The windreddened face showed a grin of faint self-mockery. "Oh, hell! It's the Fourth of July, ain't it? A man can't decently celebrate, getting drunk all by himself.

I figured this was something I wasn't laid up enough to miss."

"How's the leg?"

Flynn looked down at it in its bandage, the sock-less foot shoved into the stirrup. "I'm managing," he said. He had fashioned a crutch from a couple of pieces of wood, with rags for padding the crossbar; it was lashed behind his saddle, ready for use. Changing the subject, the mustanger said, "I guess you made it here with the string okay?"

"They're in the corral at the livery. They didn't give me too much trouble. I got my twenty dollars, and I suppose the rest was credited to your account, the way you wanted."

The eyes in the narrow face had discovered the metal pinned to Bannon's shirtfront. Flynn stabbed a calloused finger at it. "What the hell is that thing doing there?"

"The badge? I sort of fell into it," Bannon said briefly. "The town marshal found himself laid up, unexpected. One thing and another, it was decided that I'd fill in for him today."

"Sam Prentiss—laid up?" The mustanger sounded alarmed. "What happened?"

"He caught a bullet. It was more or less an accident—something like what happened to you."

"And you're fillin' in?" The shrewd eyes studied Bannon, while the horses moved uneasily with the restless stir of the holiday about them. "I thought you'd be clean over the Ochocos by this time. What of that fellow I was to watch for—the sandy-haired one, with a scar?"

"What of him?" Bannon said coldly.

At his tone the other man shrugged a bony shoulder. "Your business, I guess," he admitted. "Sure as hell ain't none of mine . . ." He lifted the rein, to ride on. "Where do I find old Sam?"

"Ashby's got him at his place. In bed."

"I crave to know just how bad hurt he is. While I'm at it, maybe I'll let the doc have a look at this dumb leg I went and perf'rated. I don't fuss much with doctors as a rule, but they do have their uses."

He gave his ugly horse a kick with his good leg; the other man watched him negotiate the spillover of traffic in front of the big, two-story hotel and disappear in the direction of Doc Ashby's place of business. Afterward, Ed Bannon turned toward the picnic ground on the flat beside the creek.

Chapter 8

A line had formed, past the barbecue pit and the long trestle tables where Mary Tracy and some of the other women of Mitchell were serving out helpings of beans and salad and coffee and slabs of homemade bread and butter. Bannon found a place to tie his horse, and as he went to queue up he glimpsed Kit Tracy, already seated on the grass in the shade. She was with some of her friends; she beckoned him to join them and he acknowledged her invitation with a nod. He collected a cup and plate, exchanged greetings with Kit's grandmother as she piled his plate high, and went over to join the group.

It included Addie Weiker and a couple of young men that Addie introduced. Bert Maroon was there as well, on the outer fringe, looking on rather morosely as the Weiker girl divided her attention among her other admirers. Bannon felt distinctly sorry for him.

Kit made room for Ed Bannon beside her on the grass. At first she seemed fairly to bubble over with high-spirited comments about one thing or another, but presently she fell silent and after that very little was said between them. Bannon managed to keep an eye on what went on around them, remembering his responsibilities; but most of all he was aware of the girl seated so close to him—wondering at her moods and sudden stillnesses, at the sometimes un-predictable and highly original turns of her thought.

Later, when he returned to the table to get their dessert, he encountered Doc Ashby carrying two plates loaded high with food. Bannon asked him, "Do you expect to eat all that?"

"Isn't for me," the doctor told him. "Cap Flynn's over at my place, with Sam Prentiss. I said I'd fetch them something from the barbecue."

"You looked at Cap's leg?"

"It's not too bad a wound, but it's painful. He seems to get around well enough on that crutch he made for himself. But Sam's restless, and it's good to have someone to keep him company. I left them playing cutthroat checkers."

With the eating nearly finished, preparations were going ahead for the next event. Bannon and Kit were too interested in their own company to be much involved. The girl laid aside her empty plate as she said, with one of her quick impulses, "Why don't we go for a walk?"

"All right. Things seem quiet enough at the moment."

They disposed of their eating utensils at the main table, and after that he let her lead the way down a path that brought them, presently, to the water's edge. They stopped here and watched the sliding and bubbling of the current through bankside growth, with the canyon's sloping walls lifting above them.

After a moment Kit said, in a hushed tone, "Do you know, sometimes I stand here listening to the creek—quiet, like this, and friendly—and I try to picture how it was the year I was born, when the flood came tearing through and swept the town away." She pointed toward the head of the canyon, where the flour mill stood and the sweep of the walls carried the upper reaches of the creek out of sight. "I've heard people try to describe what that day was like. But how could anyone even imagine it, to look at the canyon now—on a day like this?"

"It's not easy," Bannon admitted.

Together they stood listening to the creek and to a lazy hum of bees somewhere nearby. Behind them, at the picnic ground, a wagon that had served as one of the floats in that morning's parade had been pulled up and Mayor Weiker was using it for a speaker's stand, giving the crowd the benefit of his thoughts on the history and the meaning of the day they were celebrating. Bannon and the girl were aware of his voice but only an occasional word reached them, thin across the stillness. The canyon was a trough holding bright sunlight and a warm stir of breeze along the creek surface. Whatever catastrophe had happened here twenty years ago, today was no time for Ed Bannon to do anything except enjoy a pleasant moment and the nearness of this delightful girl.

Bannon stirred. It was with the feeling of ending something he didn't really want to that he said, reluctantly, "I guess I'd better get back. After all, I'm supposed to be working!"

She seemed to regret it as much as he did.

The mayor's speech was over and the musicians from the parade were taking over his place on the wagon and tuning up their instruments. A couple of wooden platforms had been brought out from somewhere and placed side by side for a dance floor. As couples began gravitating toward this, Kit Tracy turned to Bannon with eyes shining and said, "I hope you like to dance."

He hesitated. "It's not exactly my long suit."

"You could say that about any of us here in Mitchell," she assured him. "But we still have fun trying. Please!" She caught his hand and led him to the edge of the floor. Just then the fiddle struck up with "Over the Waves," the notes thin and sour above the one-two-three thump of drum and tuba. "It's a waltz," Kit said. "*Any*one can waltz." She added, "Unless, of course, you'd really rather not."

He was tempted by the thought of holding her, but hesitated to risk embarrassing both of them. Weakening, he said, "Well . . ."—and at once she smiled and lifted her arms to him.

About to step onto the floor, Bannon paused and his head turned sharply to see the horsemen jingling along Main Street toward the picnic area. They rode with style, straight up in their saddles, their animals held at an easy lope. John Luft headed them, and among the rest Bannon saw Reub Springer and others that he remembered from his mission yesterday to recover the black stud.

The JL had arrived.

From the way Kit stiffened he knew she had seen them too. He heard her say, "Oh, I just hope Reub Springer won't be looking for trouble!"

"So do I." Bannon spoke without much conviction. He and the girl both had forgotten about dancing. They stood oblivious to the activity on the platform beside them, and they watched Luft and his crew.

Some of the procession peeled off and headed for the town's saloons. The rest came on, and as they turned down toward the picnic area Bannon knew that Reub Springer had caught sight of him. There was no misreading the sudden lift of the foreman's head; even across the distance he could almost feel the intensity of the man's angry stare. He told the girl, "Maybe you'd better move away from me." But she held where she was, shaking her head without an answer, and he felt her hand move into his left hand and cling to it. Her fingers were cold and dry.

Now Luft and Springer dismounted and passed the reins of their horses up to one of the JL buckaroos to tie for them. Holiday or not, Reub Springer had come armed. Bannon saw him give the holstered gun a hitch to settle it comfortably, but when he would have started forward, his boss stopped him with a word and with an elbow lifted against him. They stood like that a moment, and they seemed to be arguing, while both their looks lay on Bannon where he stood waiting for their decision.

But Luft was not a boss who took much argument, as Bannon had already decided. He cut the redhead short and with a curt dismissal pointed out the barbecue and prodded Springer in that direction. The foreman scowled but he went, not without a last formidable look over his shoulder at Bannon. John Luft meanwhile came on across the grass, nodding brief acknowledgment of the greetings he received in passing. He came directly to Bannon and Kit, where they stood at the edge of the dance platform with the racket of the musicians pulsating behind them.

He gave Bannon a cool stare and to the girl said, "How are you, Kit?"

"Why—I'm just fine," she answered—a little stiffly, Bannon thought.

Luft nodded, the stern eyes in the strong, unhandsome face studying her. "Glad to hear it," he said in his gruff tone. Then, looking squarely at Bannon, he took in the metal badge and said without preamble, "So the report was true. We got word at the ranch that Sam Prentiss had been laid up and you were filling in for him. Got himself shot, I understand."

"You were right there when it happened," Bannon pointed out. "He took the bullet Reub Springer meant for me."

"Yes, I heard that's what you claim."

There was a muted antagonism that Bannon decided to ignore. He shrugged and said, "If you doubt my version, you can always talk to Sam."

"I just might do that. Meanwhile," the rancher said, "I've put Reub on his good behavior in town today. If there's trouble, he won't be the one to start it."

"That's good! Because I'm the one who'd have to finish it . . ."

The music for the first set had ended while they were talking. Now it started up again, interrupting whatever Luft might have answered. Instead he glanced at the couples on the floor, and then he looked at Kit Tracy and asked, with his blunt and graceless manner, "How about dancing with me?"

She was caught off guard. She shot Bannon a quick and troubled look as she hesitated. "Thank you," she said, stammering a little. "Only, I—"

There was no time to say that Ed Bannon had already been promised. For without warning, Orin Tracy was there, to sing out in his rich bass voice, "Of course she wants to dance!" A gnarled hand took Kit by the arm and shoved her at the rancher, as the old man told Luft, with a jovial wink, "Now don't you let her go coy on you, John! You know how these females act if you don't watch 'em. You just grab her and haul her out there on the floor—show her you mean business!"

Amused, Luft said, "Thanks for the tip, Orin. I guess I'll just have to do that!" And without another word being said, he had Kit in his arms and with male assurance swept her away among the other couples on the floor. Ed Bannon was left standing with her grandfather, empty-handed, to watch them go.

It was Orin Tracy who spoke, with a tone of satisfaction. "Now, there's a sight I like to see. Don't they make a real handsome couple?"

"Luft? And your granddaughter?" Bannon turned to stare at him, not sure he'd heard right. "He'd be about twice her age, wouldn't he?"

If he saw that as an objection, Tracy shrugged it aside. "Old enough to have learned some sense," he pointed out. "Old enough to have carved a place for himself in the world—and built him one of the finest ranches anywhere around this part of Oregon!"

"That's fine, of course," the younger man agreed. "For *him!* But—"

The old man didn't seem to hear. He went right on, confiding earnestly, "Bannon, there's just no way of saying how concerned I am over that girl! A body has only to count on his fingers to know that me nor her grandmother, neither one, has got that many years still coming to us. And it purely scares me to think of leaving her, without anybody or anything except a livery stable that don't earn much more than feed for the horses!

"No—before I go, the one thing I want in this world is to see her taken care of. But what chance does a girl have in a place like this? I can't see her tying herself to some common, forty-a-month buckaroo! On the other hand, to have someone as well fixed as John Luft interested in her, and to think of all the advantages it could mean— Well, you can't blame an old man for dreaming!"

Not trusting himself to answer, Bannon looked again at the pair on the dance floor—bright, dainty Kit in the arms of this bear of a man who, for all his power and distinction and the wealth of his cattle holdings, had something about him that was almost slovenly and not too clean. He thought of Luft's bachelor quarters with his crew at the JL, and he wondered: *Can Orin Tracy really picture his granddaughter as the mistress of that pigsty of a ranch?* Perhaps in his anxiety to see her taken care of, he stubbornly blinded himself to what it would actually mean—he admired John Luft as a successful rancher, and looked no further than that.

But then, Ed Bannon had to admit to himself, perhaps *he* was the one who was wrong. Maybe simple jealousy showed John Luft to him in the worst possible light, so that he could resist the thought of Kit Tracy somehow finding the man attractive . . . And with that thought came the sobering reminder: *Don't forget who you are. It's none of your business what she does!* And with that realization, he closed his mouth tightly on whatever he might have been about to say.

All at once he found he couldn't stand here any longer and watch, and without another word to Orin Tracy he turned to move away from the dance platform. As he did he happened to catch sight of young Bert Maroon standing on the sidelines, hands thrust into hip pockets and a gloomy expression on his face. Sure enough, there among the dancers was Addie Weiker, smiling up into the face of the young townsman who was her partner. Maroon's unhappy jealousy, watching the girl he fancied in the arms of another man, suddenly had Ed Bannon thinking, *Mister, I know just how you feel!*

He picked his way through the crowd and now became aware of a disturbance in another part of the picnic ground. Angry voices, tumbling over one another, reminded him that any sort of trouble today was his responsibility. He hurried to see what was going on.

It was over near the barbecue pit, where aromatic charcoal smoke still hung in low layers on the quiet air of the canyon. Bannon saw a couple of men confronting each other, while several bystanders hung about intently watching. A spilled plate of food lay in the weeds at their feet. And as Bannon neared, one of the angry pair lifted his head and he saw it was Reub Springer, in the same moment that Springer's stare locked with his.

The second man—a townsman from the look of him—appeared to be alarmed at the situation in which he found himself. His voice held a scared edge to it as he said into the dangerous stillness that had settled, "Look, Springer, I've already said it was an accident. Why would I knock a plate out of your hand on purpose?"

"You can't talk your way out of this!" But even as Reub Springer made the threat, his stare was actually on Ed Bannon, a wolfish eagerness showing as he watched the latter approaching. Now he lifted one big, rope-hard hand and let it close into a fist. "I'm gonna bust your head for you, Doolin!"

Bannon had reached the pair, shouldering through the ring of men who had clustered at the promise of a fight. He knew he was doing the very thing Springer was hoping for when he said coolly, "You're not busting anybody's head."

At once Doolin was forgotten. Reub Springer simply put out a hand and shoved him out of the way, so that he faced the man he really wanted.

"Maybe I'll break *yours*, Bannon!" the big fellow roared and started for him.

Chapter 9

Ed Bannon had hoped the authority of the badge he was wearing would have an effect, but Springer was nursing too many resentments; now he was bent on laying hands on the stranger who had twice bested him the say before.

Bannon tried a crisp warning: "No, Springer!" and he fell back a step while he started to bring out his gun.

But someone was just behind him and failed to get out of the way in time. Bannon's elbow was jammed, unable to bend or to lift. The gun was still in its holster when Reub Springer waded directly across the mess of broken plate and spilled food that had begun the trouble and barreled into him.

Already off balance, Ed Bannon was unable to get his feet sorted out and avoid the impetus of the bigger man's bull strength. Springer rushed him backward, while men yelled and scrambled to scatter out of the road. Springer's fists were working. One bounced off Bannon's shoulder, but the other caught him full on the side of the head and made it ring like a bell. And then his feet tangled and he went down as though they had been cut from under him. Reub Springer was sent stumbling over him, one heavy cowhide catching Bannon painfully in the ribs.

Partly stunned by that clout on the side of the

head, Ed Bannon managed to roll to his knees. Springer was already turning back, to come at him again. He thought once more about his gun, but the holster's sudden lack of weight told him it was empty—he had lost the gun in that spill and there wasn't time to look for it. As Bannon pushed to his feet, the shouting of voices was like a wave that rolled over the picnic ground and echoed off the canyon's sides. Vaguely he was aware that the music had broken off. Everybody in the crowd sensed a fight, and nothing else was more exciting than that.

Reub Springer had a gun but he wasn't bothering with it. Rough and tumble was his style, and his flushed features and the grin spread across his sweating face showed that he was enjoying himself. This time Springer came reaching, not hitting. Bannon tried to evade his grasp but one of those big hands caught him; his shirt ripped. Bannon used his fists but could not save himself as Reub Springer gathered him in, the thickly muscled arms trying for a hammerlock as the two of them went reeling through the scattering crowd.

When they struck the edge of one of the long serving tables, it went over with them, in a smash of spilled crockery and tinware and food. The combatants broke apart, and now Bannon felt the heat of the barbecue pit against his back and knew he had missed it by very little. He was breathing hard as he staggered up. But now he saw his hat in the trampled weeds and, near it, the shine of his lost pistol. Without hesitation he made for it and, leaning, heard the thud of Springer's boots pounding closer. He got the gun, and he turned as he brought it up and saw the big man put on the brakes, halting barely in time at the sight of the weapon pointed at his head.

Ed Bannon said tightly, "Stop right there!"

Reub Springer checked himself in midstride; the wind gusted from between his lips as he glared at the muzzle of the gun. He said harshly, "So you lost your nerve—you had to go and bring a gun into the fight!"

Bannon shook his head, his eyes cold. "Wrong, Springer! The fight was your idea. I happen to wear a badge, and all I want is to restore order." He added, "I'm putting you under arrest."

"Like hell you are!"

"I am, though. For starters, I'll ask you to take off that gun and belt and toss them over here to me."

Reub Springer merely stood there, defiant, the fingers of one big hand twitching slightly. And now Jess Weiker came hurrying, red of face and panting with exertion and alarm. Behind him came John Luft, to see what his range boss had become involved in. Without waiting to be asked, one of the bystanders told the mayor, "It was the big fellow started it, Jess. If you want my opinion, he craved a fight with somebody and he went after Bannon—for no reason or excuse to it that I could see."

"Nobody wants your opinion!" Reub Springer told the speaker loudly, but the cold looks on the faces around him would have told anyone that these on-lookers all saw matters in the same way.

Troubled, Weiker turned to his acting marshal. "Bannon?"

The latter nodded toward the bystanders. "Ask them—they'll tell you how it was. Meanwhile, I've put Springer under arrest for creating a disturbance, and I'm waiting for him to hand over his gun."

John Luft had been listening and watching, and now he stepped in with authority and a presence that wasn't to be denied. "You're going too fast, Bannon," he said sternly. "I'm aware you two have had some differences, but I won't have you taking advantage of the temporary badge you're wearing or the fact you're standing in for Sam Prentiss. I'm sorry as anyone about Sam being hurt. Since it happened at the JL, I've already told Mayor Weiker I figure to pay whatever the doc needs to see Sam back on his feet. I'll even settle for this damage." He indicated the wrecked table, the smashed and broken dishes, the food that had been spilled and wasted and trampled on.

He went on firmly: "But I need my riders—my range boss in particular. I refused to let Sam Prentiss arrest him yesterday, and I'm not letting you now." He turned to Springer and told him curtly, "I want you back at the JL, before you find your way into some real trouble. Get your horse."

Even from his own employer, Reub Springer found that kind of dismissal hard to take. He glowered, hesitating, and Ed Bannon looked at Jess Weiker for his cue. The mayor was obviously uncomfortable, reluctant to cross a man like Luft, who was, after all, important to the economy of Mitchell. He found his voice now and said hastily, "I guess there's no point making too big an issue of this— just so it don't go any further. Let him leave, Bannon. We'll take John's word that there'll be no more trouble."

"You're the boss," Bannon said and returned his gun to its holster. Reub Springer wanted to argue, but he must have seen Luft would have none of that. Frustrated, he gave his heavy shoulders a jerk and swung away, to where his friend Nick Garvey stood holding out the hat he'd lost in the fight. Others of

Springer's cronies among the saloon crowd had been there, too, to witness his humiliation. Reub Springer snatched the hat, shouldered someone out of the way, and went tramping off through the high grass.

The matter seemed settled. John Luft told the mayor, "Figure up the damage and send me a bill." Weiker promised. Sweating and harried, he set about giving orders to clean up the mess that had been created and to set things right. For a moment the rancher looked at Ed Bannon, but if he had something he wanted to say, he let it go. He turned without speaking and Bannon watched him go to join Kit Tracy and her grandparents, in the group that had hung back from the disturbance on the picnic ground.

The interruption was ended. Yonder the musicians were starting up and already people were dancing again. Ed Bannon drew a sleeve across the sweat and dirt on his face and for the first time saw the damage that had been done to his clothing. The shirt was ripped and smeared with blood—whether his own or Springer's, he didn't know—with dirt, and even food from the smashed table; he realized he would have to go and get himself cleaned up.

As he was leaning to retrieve his fallen hat, a sudden burst of hoofbeats began. He glanced up in time to see Reub Springer spurring away at an angry gallop, to pass from sight behind the buildings. The sounds faded. Bannon might have thought no one else had noticed Springer's going, but then he caught sight of Nick Garvey and his friends standing apart, a silent group. They were staring at him and he read the angry belligerence in their faces.

Ed Bannon deliberately met their look, and then he turned and headed for his horse.

The blood on the shirt was his own. He hadn't known until he peered at himself in the jail mirror that he had taken a cut on the lip. He dabbed it with cold water until the bleeding stopped; if the lip didn't swell too badly, his moustache would help to cover it. But the shirt was practically a ruin, and he was rummaging in his saddlebag for another before he remembered he no longer owned an extra one—he'd ripped it up yesterday to improvise a bandage for Sam Prentiss' bullet wound.

So all he could do at the moment was sponge the blood from his ruined shirt as best he could and then put it back on and slip his coat on over it. As he looked at the effect in the mirror, he heard the distant sound of music and thought of Kit Tracy in John Luft's arms. And he frowned, thinking of his talk with old Orin Tracy.

You really couldn't blame the old man too much, he told himself. It would be frightening to reach his age and have a young granddaughter who must somehow be provided for when his time came to leave her. Even if Bannon considered that admiration for Luft's importance and success had warped Orin Tracy's judgment in choosing a husband for her, he was hardly in a position himself to say anything. He looked at the man in the mirror—a man without even a whole shirt to his name, a man with a shadow hanging over him that made it out of the question that he should think seriously about any girl. A man who would very soon be gone from here, for good.

If John Luft had serious intentions toward Kit, he told himself bleakly, the only decent thing Ed Bannon could do was stand aside and leave the field to him . . .

So as he went outside again to his waiting horse he was grimly determined that, from here on, he would remember the fill-in job he was here to do for the ailing Marshal Prentiss. No longer did he let himself search for Kit among the people on the picnic ground or moving along the street. The rest of that interminable day he tended strictly to business—keeping to himself, and to the saddle, at an unhurried gait and hardly speaking to anyone at all. He found it surprising, after the warnings he'd had, how orderly the town was. As the day dragged out and afternoon shadows lengthened, with first lamplight beginning to glow along the canyon, there were a couple of brief disturbances but these were caused by buckaroos who had taken on too much to drink and who subsided readily enough when Bannon gave them a warning. He began to wonder if the showing he'd made by standing up to Reub Springer might have had its effect.

Full night settled. At this season of the year, the sky didn't completely darken until nine; but long before that, the picnic ground, the porch of the hotel, and the front yards of houses up on Piety Hill blossomed with colored fire. He saw Roman candles and pinwheels, figure eights drawn by sparklers in the hands of kids, and now and then the bright scratch of a skyrocket arcing across the stars. As he watched, the knowledge that he was an outsider who had no real part in all this settled on Ed Bannon and presently dropped him into a melancholy mood that came close to lonely self-pity.

But that in turn made him angry. No point in getting mawkish, he told himself, over a girl he couldn't have or because of the reminders of other Independence Days in a small town in Illinois, and a youngster there who'd wanted nothing so much as to get away—to see something wider than the horizons of village life.

So what was there about Mitchell, Oregon, with its population of perhaps two hundred people, that it should hold him now?

The evening passed somehow. The fireworks were shot and eventually the last scintillating streaks of red and white and green died and vanished. The carbide cannon that had been putting its explosive echoes through the canyon at intervals all day long was fired off for the last time, and after that only an occasional firecracker still sounded in the deepening night. Tomorrow would be simply another work day. The life along Main Street began to thin out as buckaroos got their horses and struck out for scattered ranches and the men of the town left off celebrating and climbed the hill to their homes.

Toward midnight, Ed Bannon judged that he was over the hump and that, from this point on, things would be winding down.

At the corner where Nelson Street dropped steeply down to enter Main, something moved in a building's shadow and he instinctively drew rein while his hand sought the butt of his holstered revolver. But then wood thumped the sidewalk and a man moved out into better view, and he saw that it was Cap Flynn, homemade crutch under his arm. He spoke Bannon's name in a hoarse whisper and brought him over to look down at him from the saddle.

"I been waiting for you," the mustanger said

without preface. "Some minutes ago I noticed two-three fellows scouting around the jail, making mighty little fuss about it. I haven't seen 'em leave. I got an idea they're waiting, too."

Bannon heard this with a feeling of inevitability, as if it were something he had known was bound to come. He moved the horse around a little, so he could put a glance up the darkened side street toward the jail whose squat, whitewashed shape showed dimly. "Two of them, you said?"

"*Or* three. I think maybe three." Cap Flynn shifted his weight on the crossbar of the crutch. "You done me a favor, couple of days ago," he said roughly. "I ain't too spry just now, with this dumb leg. But if I can—"

Bannon cut him off. "Thanks all the same. Don't worry about this. I'll handle it."

"If you say so." The old mustanger stayed where he was, watching the other man, trying to read his face in the darkness. Ed Bannon, considering the problem, had already decided the only thing was to meet it directly. Abruptly he neck-reined his horse and started up the steep pitch of Nelson Street, riding openly and without hesitation. Behind him he heard Flynn stump out into the street where he could watch.

Bannon searched the shadows but could see nothing that looked like a man lurking in wait for him. It was only an effect of nerves, but the night seemed to hold its breath. Somewhere a firecracker popped distantly, making him wonder who it was that had found one last firecracker to set off.

He climbed the hundred feet or so and then, not having detected any warning movement or sound, turned in on the uphill side of the jail and dismounted. When he took the bridle and started to lead his animal toward the horse shed at the back of the lot, he was careful to put the dun between him and the faint glimmer of whitewash that was the jail building. He reached the shed without incident, removed the piece of stick which was thrust through the hasp of the shed door, and swung the door open. Within, Sam Prentiss' animal stomped once.

Bannon gave the dun a light slap on the rump, enough to send it on into the dark interior, and at the same moment faded around the shed's outside corner. There Bannon put his shoulder against the clapboard and drew his gun. He waited like that, unconsciously holding his breath. The night wind plucked at his clothing and once again a firecracker exploded, somewhere in the distance. Incongruously, Ed Bannon had another flash of recollection: A small boy lying in his bed, sleepily trying to make himself stay awake so he could count the last one and never sure that he succeeded . . .

Now a dark figure separated itself from the shadows piled against the jail wall, eased into the open and halted there, uncertain—having been fooled into thinking Bannon had led the horse inside, he would be starting to wonder why there was no sound of the dun being unsaddled. Beginning to grow bolder, the man drifted forward toward the shed door, and Bannon caught the faint gleam of a rifle barrel.

He let the man almost reach the dark opening before he said quietly, "Over here, Garvey."

The figure made a convulsive movement. The rifle

started to lift and Bannon warned, "Don't try to use that! My gun's pointed right at you—you'd better freeze!" Nick Garvey froze. There was no move or sound of protest when Bannon walked over and took the long gun from unresisting hands. "Now," he ordered, "call in your friends."

Garvey hesitated, yet there was no way he could refuse. He drew an audible breath and called, in a shaky voice, "All right, Harry! Jeff! The sonofabitch got me. You two come on in!"

Ed Bannon was hardly surprised when they didn't. There came instead the sudden noise of a couple of men breaking into a run, footsteps scurrying off down the hill. These quickly faded and Bannon was left alone with his prisoner. He commented dryly, "Brave fellows!"

Garvey didn't answer. He was breathing hoarsely, like a man very much afraid.

Ed Bannon hefted the weapon he'd taken from him and asked, "Is this your rifle or did you borrow it?" He looked at Garvey. "Well, no matter. I'll hold it at the jail until it's called for."

Nick Garvey found his voice. "You locking me up?"

"Any reason I shouldn't? This was meant to square things, I suppose, for what happened to Springer today." He went on gruffly, without waiting for an answer, "It's late, and I don't feel like bothering with you. How I'll feel in the morning, I don't know. You'd better get along before I change my mind!"

He nudged the man with the muzzle of the captured rifle. Nick Garvey needed no urging; he took off at a run. Bannon holstered his revolver and, still holding the rifle, stood listening to him go.

A night wind moved through the canyon, bringing him the voice of the creek in its channel and a tang of sage and juniper from the wild land beyond. It almost began to feel as though his first day of duty as a substitute marshal was actually over.

Chapter 10

By morning, Nick Garvey was gone from Mitchell.

Bannon learned of this when he looked in at Chipman's and got the word from the saloonkeeper himself. "Somebody saw him ride out a little past midnight, him and that pair he generally hangs around with—Jeff Pitts and Harry Ruser. They never said where they was headed."

"Some people," Ed Bannon observed, "would probably be just as pleased if they were to keep right on going."

"I don't count on it," Chipman said sourly. "They always turn up again. This is the busy time of year— they might even take a job buckarooing somewhere and be back as soon as they've got some more drinking money together. It's their style."

Bannon had his own theory, that the spoiling of last night's ambush at the jail might have convinced those three that Mitchell wasn't a good place for them just now. He let the matter rest. He refused the drink Chipman offered him, saying it was too early in the day for him. A moment afterward, he left.

Mitchell had scarcely begun to rouse itself. Empty and still, it didn't look like the same town as yesterday. This morning, it was as though a storm had swept through, littering the street and the picnic ground along the creek with trash that someone would have the pleasure of cleaning up. Bannon walked the few steps to Ashby's place and knocked on the casing beside the open door.

Doc Ashby let him in and passed him, without comment, into the room where Sam Prentiss lay. Sam's color looked better this morning; mostly he appeared bored. He was looking at the illustrations in one of Ashby's thick medical books. He laid the book aside, saying, "Glad you dropped in. This damn book scares the hell out of me! I had no idea so many things could go wrong with the human body."

Ed Bannon told him, "You sound like *you're* feeling better at least."

"Mending is a pretty slow business." The marshal shifted position a little and winced. "*You* look a mite the worse for wear," he commented shrewdly, staring at the lopsided swelling on Bannon's upper lip. "And it appears I owe you another shirt. Reub Springer, eh?"

"You heard?"

"I heard about him starting a fight that near busted up the celebration, except for you putting him in his place. In fact, I've been hearing practically nothing else!" Prentiss wagged his head against the pillow. "That was a good piece of work—only, you should have jailed him while you were at it, instead of just posting him out of town."

Bannon said, "Tell that to your mayor. When he gave the orders, I hadn't much choice but to follow them."

"I guess that's so. And of course, Jess Weiker will never do anything contrary to what John Luft wants—the JL is his biggest customer. Still, I was pleased to hear Springer got put in his place.

"Ain't *all* I heard, though," the lawman went on. "I got the damndest yarn out of Cap Flynn this morning, before he left for that starve-out he calls a mustanger outfit. He told me some gents tried to lay for you at the jail, then took off like scalded cats when you showed up—and not even a shot fired. Just what about that?"

Bannon had been wondering how much Flynn might have seen last night of the results of his warning. He said only, "As you say, it was nothing—some of Reub Springer's friends, the same trio I had to disarm the other evening. They had something in mind, all right, but they thought better of it. I since hear they've left town."

"Cleaning house, eh?" Prentiss nodded, approving. "All in all, I'd say you've more than done the job I was hoping you would. I'm glad I thought of offering you that badge. Now the holiday's over with, things should be quiet again. It's all right with me whenever you decide to unpin that thing and ride on out of here."

Ed Bannon considered a moment, then shook his head. "Could be a little early, yet. You're still a long way from mended. Maybe I better stick around a spell longer."

The sharp eyes in the wrinkled face studied him. Sam Prentiss said bluntly, "Don't that sound like shaving things a little thin? Not leaving, now you got the chance?"

Bannon knew what he was referring to. His face was a mask as he said, "It's not your worry. You stay there till the doc says you'll be all right on your feet. I can look after my own affairs. Anyway"—and the mask eased a little as his swollen lip beneath the thick moustache managed a smile—"I've got some

unfinished business here at Mitchell. No, not Reub
Springer—he means nothing at all, far as I'm concerned. But there's the black stud, for one thing. I
have a lot of respect for that animal; I'd like to see
what can be done with him.

"I'll be staying a day or so, anyway. You go on
reading your book and getting mended. I'll let you
know if I decide my time's come to leave . . ."

Bannon crossed Main Street and stepped for a
moment into Weiker's Emporium. As he expected, it
proved to be one of those places where the people of
a small town could buy almost anything, from clothing to hardware—he saw bins full of boots and shoes
and stacks of ready-made trousers and women's
blouses, tin pails and rakes and brooms and even a
case, fronted with polished glass, that held a display
of handguns and hunting knives.

Bert Maroon was showing a couple of towns-
women some yard goods, but he could hardly wait
to leave them standing while he came hurrying, eager to see what he could do for Bannon. He had witnessed the fight with Reub Springer, of course, and
he wanted to talk about it. Bannon cut him off rather
abruptly, reminding him he had customers already
waiting.

He didn't enjoy hurting the young fellow's
feelings—Bert Maroon got more than enough of
that at the flirtatious hands of Addie Weiker—but to
be treated with hero worship was uncomfortable
and embarrassing. He had come for shirts; he
picked out a couple that should fit him, paying cash.
As he left the store and headed for the barbershop,
to have a bath and get his thick black mane trimmed
into some kind of shape, he found himself admitting
what others had discovered before him—that flattery,

especially when undeserved, could be too pleasant for most men's good . . .

When Kit Tracy came down off the hill that morning she stopped by the jail, looking for Bannon. He didn't seem to be around, though his saddlebags were there and his rifle was leaning against the wall near the neatly made-up cot where he had slept. Thoughtful and admittedly disappointed, she went on to the stable and there found Howie Whipple already at his interminable task of cleaning out the stalls.

The new horses were in the corrals, the black stud in a pen to himself. She paused to look at him for a moment, as he moved restlessly about within his prison. She was still standing there in the sun when Howie came to her, frowning over something.

"This has been sort of chewing at me, ever since yesterday," he told her. "It just seemed funny, that's all. I been wanting to tell somebody."

"Oh?" she said, idly, wishing to encourage him but still immersed in her own thoughts.

Howie went on, "I did kind of think he wanted it kept quiet. On the other hand, he didn't really *say* I wasn't to mention it . . ."

Really aware of what she was hearing, Kit turned in some impatience. "Mention what, Howie? Who is it we're talking about?"

"Why, *you* know. That new fella—"

"Mr. Bannon?" He nodded. Really concerned now, she exclaimed, "You'd better tell me the rest. What did he say that's bothering you?"

"It was something he asked me to do for him— somebody he wanted me to keep an eye out for. If this man should show up, maybe asking after Bannon, I wasn't to say nothing but then let Bannon know right away. Don't that sound kind of funny to you?"

She was staring at him. She managed to answer, "I can't see it has to mean anything. Could be some friend he's supposed to meet and doesn't want to take a chance of missing."

"But then, why ain't I supposed to tell the gent he's here?"

"Well—oh, I don't know, Howie!" She knew how lame her argument sounded. In her heart a suspicion had been planted and she found herself gone cold all over. "Did he give this man a name?"

Howie shook his head. "Described him, though. Fair complected, he said, and mentioned a scar I'd see on the fellow's cheek. Hey, you won't tell Bannon I said nothing to you?" he added, anxiously. "He might be mad—and I don't think I'd want him mad at me!"

"Of course I won't tell," she assured him. "But don't *you* say anything to anyone else; we'll keep this our secret—all right?" She waited until he nodded agreement. "But if that man *should* happen to show up—or somebody that looks like it might be him—you be sure and let me know, won't you?"

"Sure," Howie told her, and she left it there.

An hour later, when she was seated in the cubbyhole office filling out an order from a harness catalogue but with only a part of her mind on what she was doing, through the window she heard a sound of voices that made her raise her head and listen. She tried resolutely to continue with her work, but after a moment she gave in to the concern that was bothering her. She put down the pen, pushed order sheet and catalogue from her, and, getting to her feet, went out through the shadowy barn interior and into the sunshine.

Howie Whipple and Ed Bannon stood by the bars of the stud's pen, watching the black as he moved about in there and stirred the dust with unshod hooves. As Kit approached them their brief conversation ended and Howie turned away about his chores; Bannon saw the girl, then. For just a moment she wondered if, for some unknown reason, he meant to walk away, pretending he hadn't noticed her. But he held where he was and let her come up to where he stood, trying to read the expression on his face. He nodded, unsmiling. She had an inescapable feeling that he would have avoided the meeting if he could; this puzzled her and made her all the more determined.

"Hello!" she said with forced cheeriness. "I've been wondering about you. I didn't see you anymore yesterday, after the dancing started—and after you had that trouble with Reub Springer. It was as though you disappeared somewhere. I got to thinking you might be hurt."

"Oh, no," he said. "Nothing worse than a cut lip— I don't know what I did to Springer. Anyway, I found things to keep me busy the rest of the evening. After all, I was on duty, you know."

"Well, *that's* over, anyway. The Fourth of July, I mean. But you're still standing in for Sam Prentiss?"

He nodded. "Looks sort of like it. Ashby isn't going to let him out of that bed for awhile yet."

Kit considered that, thoughtfully gnawing at her lower lip. After what Howie Whipple had told her, she could only wonder more than ever at this strange man and at the unknown danger suggested by the nameless man with the scar. This knowledge that she couldn't speak of was like a wall suddenly risen between them.

Bannon had turned again to look at the black horse. She studied the strong profile, turned partly from her. He looked different—she realized that the ragged ends of hair that almost brushed his collar had been neatly and professionally trimmed back; it greatly improved his appearance, without in any way detracting from its strength. She was so absorbed in the puzzle of the man that he had to repeat a question before she realized he had changed the subject: "Has your grandfather decided what he plans to do with the stud?"

"Not that I know of. I think he plans to let the others go when he can, in a quick sale, just to get them off his hands. But the black won't be part of it."

"I hope not. He's too good an animal to be wasted."

Kit gave her own attention to the black, which had drawn back from the fence and was watching them, ears forward, intelligent eyes alert.

Bannon said, "It would be a shame to turn him over to some ordinary bronc-stomper. That kind only knows how to use the whip and the spur and ride him into the ground—or try to—over and over, until he either breaks his spirit or turns him into an outlaw, no use to anybody. Cap Flynn's already topped him off two or three times since he caught him—that can't have done any good."

Kit exclaimed, "I think you really must have worked with horses."

"Some," he admitted. "I know one thing—I'd certainly like to see what I can do with this one."

"Then why don't you?" He looked at her. "Maybe there isn't time enough, but if you feel like trying, I know it would be all right with Grandpa. And if you did have any luck and want the black for yourself, he'd probably make you a good deal on him."

Something in the suggestion caused him to smile. "If I have any luck with him," he pointed out, as though amused, "I don't know if I could afford what he'd be worth! And that wasn't the point. It's just that I hate to see a good piece of horseflesh ruined, if there's any way I can prevent it!"

She clapped her hands together. "But I think it would be wonderful! He'll be right here, anytime you might want to work with him."

Bannon found himself starting to take to the idea, but he had an objection. "It could never work if it means having the whole town looking on, bothering him. I only wish there was somewhere I could get him alone, with nobody to interfere."

"Why, I know just the place," Kit told him. "An old public corral, out on the flats the other side of the creek—not more than an hour's ride from town. Nobody uses it much. I can take you there; I'd love to see how you intend to work with him—that is, if *I* won't be in the way."

A grin softened the rugged shape of his face. "You'd never be in the way. Maybe this afternoon, for an hour or so? I can't say it looks as if I'm going to be exactly busy."

"This afternoon," Kit agreed, delighted. And it was arranged.

When Bannon rode his dun horse to the stable at the appointed time, Kit was saddled and ready. Her riding clothes consisted of a blouse and jacket and half boots and a divided skirt, with a wide-brimmed hat atop her curls. Bannon thought she looked very attractive but she startled him a little, too. He was not accustomed to seeing a woman sit astride a horse, but she seemed to think it the most natural thing in the world.

Bannon roped the stud, despite all the black's clever attempts to avoid the loop. He deftly snubbed him down and fashioned a blindfold from his neck-cloth. This subdued the animal and held him, trembling, until Bannon could put the halter on, talking in friendly tones. The blindfold was removed, and in a few minutes they were setting off down the canyon with the stud allowing himself to be led after some initial dispute.

Kit, mounted on a high-spirited little chestnut mare, said, "Grandpa was in, a while ago. I told him what you meant to do and he wished you luck."

"He doesn't mind, then?"

"Oh, not at all. If you've got the patience to try doing something with the black, it suits him fine. I told him you were a real expert."

"You don't know that."

"Maybe I fibbed a little. But I think I know enough about horses to recognize someone else who does when I see him!"

About an hour later they turned away from the Bridge Creek canyon along a wagon track into the dry hills and presently reached the corral the girl had spoken of. It was built against a flinty hillside, with a snubbing post in its center and a seep spring feeding a trickle of water into a wooden trough. The corral looked seldom used, but when Bannon gave the timbers a shake and found them tight and sturdy enough, he pronounced it adequate.

The stud tried to avoid going through the gate, having learned by now that he didn't like corrals, but Bannon would stand for no nonsense. Even so, the dun had to all but drag him in, the black neck stretched and hooves gouging up the yellow dust, and once inside the black changed tactics and tried to kick the other horse's head in, squealing his anger. The dun avoided him with the quick movements of a trained stock pony, and Bannon was able to drop a few loops of the lead rope over the snubbing post, tying it off high to prevent the animal from injuring himself in his vain attempts to pull free. The black came tearing around the post, throwing his heels. Bannon spun his own mount out of the way and through the gate, which Kit closed behind them. The prisoner was left alone awhile, to cool off and think things over.

As they stood watching him, Kit said suddenly, "Oh, I almost forgot—you're invited to supper."

Bannon showed his surprise. "You mean to-night?"

"Grandma insists. She won't believe a decent meal was ever got at any restaurant. She wants you at our place, five-thirty sharp."

"It's very nice of her, but isn't she afraid of turning me into a sponger? I certainly don't expect your people to feed me."

"Well, I've given you the message. I'd advise you to be there."

He stretched his swollen lip in a smile. "Oh, I mean to. Having eaten one of her meals, I wouldn't miss it for anything . . ."

It was time to get back to the job at hand.

Ed Bannon had already decided that he had one advantage, in that he and the black were not really strangers. The horse knew the sight and the smell of him and had felt his touch when Bannon rubbed him down after the bout with Cap Flynn in the mustanger's breaking corral. Though they had fought each other on the towrope all those miles to Mitchell, he had never done the animal any actual hurt and the stud had sense enough to know it— even if not a friend, this man had shown himself to be a fair adversary. Now Bannon set out to make the horse accept him.

He eased between the bars, moving casually and trying to avoid arousing suspicions. Inside, he straightened and leaned his shoulders against the fence and studied the black, which was aware of him and watching him in turn with wild eyes. Bannon began to talk to him—not saying anything in particular, merely keeping up a pleasant and reassuring monotone. And as he did, he started edging forward.

At once the black tried to lunge away but with the rope holding him all he managed to do was circle the post, effectively winding himself up; very quickly he was brought up short with his nose against it and unable to go any farther. He stood trembling, stomping one hoof, as Bannon closed in and placed a hand on the smoothly muscled shoulder.

The hide twitched, but the horse had felt his touch before and endured it now. "Good boy!" Ed Bannon said. "We're doing fine here, aren't we?"

Still talking, Bannon began to stroke the horse, passing his hand along the shoulder, over the withers, and along the sleek back. He half expected the animal to explode, to try to get at him with those strong teeth or the edge of a hoof. But it failed to happen and he kept on as he was, unhurried, for long and patient minutes, letting the tone of his voice and the reassuring touch of his hands work for him.

Finally, when the time seemed right, he took from a pocket of his coat certain ammunition with which he'd equipped himself before he left town—an ear of sweet corn. He held it out but at first the black spurned it, snorting and walling his eyes.

"Oh, come on, now," Bannon chided him. "What's acting like that going to get you? You like this good stuff—no point trying to tell me you don't!"

Gingerly, suspiciously, the black reached for the ear of corn while Bannon waited, to snatch his fingers clear as the big teeth closed on it. The horse munched noisily and Kit Tracy, watching from the fence, gave a crow of triumph, "Now you've got him eating out of your hand."

"Pass me the blanket."

She had been instructed to have a saddle blanket ready. Bannon went and got it from her, keeping the thing down and inconspicuous because he knew any flapping piece of cloth was more than enough to spook a nervous horse. Returning with it he proceeded to rub the blanket lightly over the animal's legs and across his chest. The black, still working on the ear of corn, scarcely appeared to notice when, with a deft move, Bannon slid the blanket into place across his back and smoothed it out there.

Kit Tracy asked, "Do you want the saddle?"

"I think not," Bannon said. "He's had enough for one session. The main thing I want is for him to remember I've never done anything to hurt him . . . and if possible, to get the idea I'm somebody it might be worth his while to know better. Here," he told the black and reached again toward his pocket.

This time the horse didn't have to be invited to stretch his neck for the offering. "You learn fast, don't you, fellow!" With something like real affection, Bannon slapped the satiny neck, while the cheek muscles bulged and the corn was devoured amid satisfied crunchings.

"Time to head back," Ed Bannon said. "I don't like to overdo it. Besides, I've been away from my job long enough—wouldn't want the town falling apart. We'll try again tomorrow—all right?"

"Oh, yes!" cried Kit. "And tomorrow you'll be able to ride him, sure!" She clearly believed it.

Chapter 11

Supper at the Tracys', with late sunlight pouring golden through the curtained windows, was to Bannon's thinking almost as substantial as Sunday dinner had been—meat stew this time, with fresh-baked bread and jam and watermelon pickles and a full array of side dishes, and sliced fresh peaches and an angel food cake to finish the meal. Kit, who had been nearly silent on the other occasion, now all but monopolized the conversation. She wanted to talk about the black stud and about Ed Bannon's initial success in breaking past the barrier of wildness and gaining confidence.

"That horse is *so* smart!" she insisted, almost forgetting to eat in her enthusiasm. "You can tell from the look of his eye. And before you know it, Ed's going to have him tamed. It's really amazing, how he knows just the right things to do."

Bannon found this most embarrassing; his performance with the black hadn't been all that impressive. And then he glanced at Orin Tracy and found the old man eying him with a face gone gravely stern. Something warned him that, for reasons of his own, Kit's grandfather did not much like what he was hearing and that it made him look on their guest with new misgivings. This troubled Bannon and took the edge off his enjoyment of the meal in this pleasant room.

Afterward, while Kit helped her grandmother clear the table, Bannon found himself on the porch with the old man. They stood observing the slanted light that fell on houses and trees and on picket fences enclosing the burgeoning gardens of Mitchell. Neither man spoke at first. Orin Tracy was fashioning a hand-rolled cigarette with fingers that were brown-stained from years at that occupation. All his attention on what he was doing, he said suddenly, "Our girl seems right well taken with you, Mr. Bannon."

Bannon looked at the old man, trying to read the thought behind his frown. He answered carefully, "She loves horses. In a country such as this, she sees them mistreated a lot. I think it just gives her pleasure when somebody takes a gentle hand to one."

"Hmm. Maybe." Tracy licked the twisted paper and punched it into shape, shoved it into the middle of his white bush of beard. He dug up a kitchen match from his pocket and scraped it into flame against a roof support. "Well," he said, the cigarette bobbing between his lips, "I'll be honest with you— and hope you will with me." He lit up, blew out a blue gust of smoke as he tossed the match aside. He plucked the twist of paper and tobacco from his mouth and looked at the burning end. "You know my feelings. Nothing in this world is important to me any more outside of her and seeing her happy and provided for."

Bannon nodded. "Yes, that's what you said. In your place I'd feel exactly the same."

"Glad to hear it. Because you must understand,

I'm kind of concerned about you, Bannon." Orin Tracy wagged his head, his mouth and eyes bleakly serious. "Three days ago our Katherine never so much as laid eyes on you or heard your name. But that's all changed. Just now, listening to her talk, for the first time I had a hint of what your being here has gone and done.

"Understand, I got nothing against you personal. I don't even know you. In fact, that's just the trouble: I don't feel like I know who you are, where you come from—or how long it will take to finish whatever it is you're doing here. And I got to say I don't appreciate having to see you turn Katherine's world upside down, and all my hopes and plans for her."

Ed Bannon said bluntly, "Your plans concerning John Luft, you mean. Well, I suppose whatever you're thinking about me is probably pretty close to true. I own no big ranch. There's maybe thirty dollars in my pocket, including what I was paid for delivering that bunch of wild scrubs for Cap Flynn. I mean to stay here only as long as it takes Sam Prentiss to get his feet under him again. As for your granddaughter, hurting her in any way is the last thing in the world I'd think of doing. Is that honest enough for you?"

Tracy puffed furiously. "It will have to do, I guess," he grunted finally. "But as for not hurting her— Damn it, she's too young! Best thing you could do would be to promise you'll stay clear away from her!"

"In a town no bigger than Mitchell," Bannon said gruffly, "that ain't too easily arranged. And I won't make anyone—not even you—a promise I ain't sure I can keep!"

From the sharp tilting of the old man's head, Ban-

non knew he hadn't liked that answer; but he didn't
know any other he could have given.

The first reaction was one of anger and resentment,
but that was a luxury he could enjoy for no longer
than it took to admit the old man had been right—
more right, in fact, than he could have any way of
knowing. There were things about Ed Bannon of
which no one here had been given any inkling.
Suddenly he felt trapped—by his commitment to
Sam Prentiss, by his own past, by the feeling he had
discovered for Kit Tracy, and by her evident feeling
for him.

That evening he left the Tracys' as quickly as he
could, using as an excuse his evening chores of
checking locks and looking into the temper of
things along Main Street. But he didn't get away
without a reminder from Kit of their date the next
day for another session with the black. Bannon
caught Orin Tracy's stern look across the girl's
shoulder. However, a promise was a promise and he
assured her he wouldn't forget.

Still, it gave him a restless night with his problems, and when he arrived at the stable the next
afternoon the first person he saw was Orin Tracy.
The old man stiffened with displeasure at sight of
him. Tracy stood in the wide doorway with hands
thrust into hip pockets, eying Ed Bannon as though
he would use his own wasted frame to prevent him
entering. But as Bannon rode up and stepped from
the saddle, Kit herself came hurrying out, smiling a
warm greeting. She was dressed the same as yesterday, and he saw her little chestnut mare already saddled and waiting, tied to a post of the corral that
held the black.

Apparently Kit was unaware of her grandfather's scowl as she took Bannon's arm and swung along beside him toward the corral, with the dun trailing. He already had an ear of sweet corn ready; the stud had been expecting it and came over to the fence without hesitatio. "You wouldn't be greedy, would you?" Bannon commented, amused. The stud, busy munching, let him slip the halter into place with hardly more than a brief, protesting toss of the head.

Kit said, "You'll ride him today, won't you?"

"That's up to him. No need to rush things."

He settled the halter and attached the lead rope. He was about to turn and mount the dun when he heard Kit exclaim, "Why, what on earth is this coming?" He turned his head to look. An odd cavalcade had just moved into view along the lower canyon, four riders approaching at an easy pace escorting a very strange-looking vehicle. The girl cried out suddenly, "Oh, Ed! Look! I've never seen a horseless carriage before!"

"It's horseless, all right."

Aside from that, it could have been a spanking-new topless buggy, its shining, red-trimmed coat of black paint filmed with dust raised by the spinning wire wheels. Enthroned on padded leather, John Luft held the tiller as he might the reins of an elegant pair of matched bays, while the single-cylinder engine in the covered box behind the seat maintained a steady sputtering. Along with his escort of buckaroos he took the shallow creek crossing, and as he neared the stable every horse in sight or sound of his vehicle started to go crazy.

Bannon managed to catch the headstalls of the dun and of Kit's little chestnut and keep them settled; oddly enough, only the black stud seemed to keep his head amid the sharp squeals and pound of hooves. Luft had braked down in front of the stable, his buckaroos reining in. It was as though the village had come awake all at once, from the way a mass of men and boys came streaming down the curve of Main Street to see this marvel. Luft gave a condescending nod to Orin Tracy who had come hurrying forward.

"Great day in the morning, John!" the old man exclaimed. "When on earth did you get that?"

"Took delivery last evening," the rancher said. "A man drove it down from The Dalles for me—the first horseless carriage in Wheeler County—in all eastern Oregon, far as I know. It's an Oldsmobile curved-dash runabout. One cylinder, chain drive, two forward and reverse speeds, epicyclic gear change . . ." Evidently he had been reading the literature that came with it. "Set me back six hundred fifty, plus freight charges from Detroit. The horn came extra." It was mounted on the tiller, and he demonstrated with a squawk from the bulb that set the horses going again.

Orin Tracy showed a mixture of admiration, envy, and mistrust of a machine that would compete with a horse. Like his granddaughter and the rest of the crowd, he had never actually seen one of the new vehicles before. He inspected the trim lines of the little buggy, with its leaf springs and its curving floorboards that curled up to form the dash, a coal-oil lantern mounted at either side. "What sort of speed can you get?" he wanted to know.

"It's supposed to do up to twenty miles an hour, if there was such a thing as a decent stretch of road in this country." Luft had been hunting about and now he caught sight of Kit, standing with Bannon at the corral. He touched his hat to her, let a cool stare rest a moment on the man beside her, and told Orin Tracy, "I was thinking your granddaughter might enjoy taking a little spin, to see how it rides."

"Why, certainly!" Tracy turned, beckoning. "Girl, get over here. You're going to get a ride in Mr. Luft's brand-new horseless buggy!"

To Bannon she did not seem at all enthusiastic. She hung back, and he could see the stiff set of her shoulders. Orin Tracy, with quick impatience, gestured again and called, more loudly, "Didn't you hear, girl? John ain't going to wait all day—and when will you get another chance like this? Now, come along!"

With so many eyes on her, all jealous of her opportunity, she could scarcely argue. She threw Bannon a hopeless glance and shake of head and left him. She had never said it, but watching her accept Luft's hand-up and settle in place beside him, Bannon knew suddenly that she felt an active dislike, perhaps even some trace of fear, of John Luft.

Her first ride in an automobile should have been a thrill and an adventure, but not with her grandfather determinedly throwing her at a man she plainly didn't like. Now Luft threw off the brake and, with another toot of the horn and his hand firm on the tiller, sent his automobile put-putting up the street to the rhythmic stroke of its single-cylinder engine, his escort of buckaroos following and the locals streaming and yelling alongside, while the few horses along the hitching rails bucked at their tethers in a frenzy. Kit, on the high leather seat, looked small and forlorn beside the rancher's arrogant shape. Bannon felt suddenly sorry for her.

And then he saw Orin Tracy looking at him, saw

the old man's satisfaction in separating Bannon and his granddaughter. Bannon returned the look, gritting his teeth. Afterward, Orin Tracy walked back into the livery barn and Ed Bannon, turning, threw himself into the saddle. He jerked open the gate, got the rope fastened to the black's halter, and started off down the canyon road leading the stud, angry emotions working in him.

He would have done better to forgo a session with the black, as soon became clear once he reached the breaking corral and turned the horse into it. He was too concerned and upset about Kit and about his own inability to do anything to change the situation; it put him in a mood and the sensitive animal reacted to it. Bannon could seem to do nothing with him, which further shortened his temper and made matters worse, both man and horse turning stubborn. Bannon had got it in his head that today, following up his success the day before, he was going to get the saddle on; the black was just as determined that he should not. Bannon got the blanket in place, but when he approached carrying the heavy stock saddle the black went wild. Twice, swearing and angry, he managed to get it slung onto the wide barrel; both times it was bucked and flung into the dirt.

Finally, after half an hour of trying to maneuver the animal into accepting the heavy construction of wood and leather, Ed Bannon had to admit he was going at it wrong and undoing what he'd already accomplished. The second time a lashing hoof narrowly missed braining him he dropped the saddle and, breathing hard, smeared sweat and dust across his cheeks with a sleeve while he stared at his adversary.

"All right," he said gruffly. "This is all my fault. Let's start over . . ."

Kit rode out from town toward the breaking corral, through the slanting light of late afternoon. It looked deserted; the pole gate had been left standing open, when by range courtesy anyone who used this pen always was careful to close it afterward. Puzzled, almost alarmed, she was nearly at the corral before a movement in the shadow of a tall juniper took her eye and then she saw Bannon's dun horse standing, saddleless, tied to the rough-barked trunk. She drew rein, frowning, and lifted herself in the stirrups for a long look around the silent, brush-strewn flat.

Sunlight lay upon the stillness, wind moved the sage and whistled a faint organ note in the cap rock of a shouldering hill. A hawk circled up there, wings spread against the blue, and slid from sight behind the lava rim; it was the only movement. As she considered, Kit pulled off her hat and let the warm breeze rough her hair. Afterward she stepped down, to see if she could find sign to tell her anything.

At that moment she caught a sound of hooves and, lifting her head, saw a horse and rider coming across the flat. She waited and they grew larger, moving in at a steady, ground-eating lope. Even before she could see either distinctly she knew, somehow, that they were Bannon and the black stud. Minutes later they came to a halt in front of her and Kit, clapping her hands, was saying, "You did it! You're riding him!"

"No trouble at all," Bannon said. "Once you figure out how to deal with him. He's a real good horse."

Everything was in place—bridle, saddle, and bit. Horse and man were both sweating and layered with dust, but if there had been a fight, neither showed any sign of it. The stud's ears were alert and he was tonguing the unfamiliar bit, trying to get used to it. Now Bannon dropped from saddle and slipped the bit, and at once the black began searching for a handout of the sweet corn he'd learned by now to expect.

Kit said, her brow creasing, "But, I didn't get to watch it! You never waited for me."

"Looked like you were going to be otherwise occupied," Ed Bannon pointed out, "so I had to come by myself. How was your auto ride?"

"All right, I suppose."

When she didn't seem inclined to elaborate, he pressed her for details, watching her face closely. "That all you can say for it? Where did Luft take you?"

"Out the old stage road a mile or two. The ruts were kind of rough going, on those narrow wheels. Finally I asked him to turn around and he did." She looked at Bannon directly. "Ed, did you suppose it was my *choice* to go with him today—instead of coming here with you?"

He answered seriously. "I wouldn't have blamed you, if it had been—I've heard so much about them, I wouldn't mind seeing how those machines operate myself. But it seemed pretty clear this was mostly your grandfather's notion."

Kit nodded unhappily. "Grandpa's just too anxious about me! Afraid I'll end up an old maid, I guess—that I won't be 'taken care of,' as he puts it. Oh, he's a dear—but all the same, he can't seem to think of anything except that I should marry John Luft!"

"And you don't see it that way?"

"No! Oh, I don't know anything against him," she

went on, flinging out her hands as though in despair of making herself clear. "But I—I couldn't *marry* him! For one thing, I simply don't like the kind of men he has riding for him. Grandpa says that shouldn't mean anything, but to me it does. They're more than just his hired hands—he's *one* of them. Any woman who marries him will have to get used to living out on that ranch of his, alone in the midst of that tough crew!" She seemed to shudder at the thought. "In spite of Grandpa, I just won't encourage him. I don't know why he doesn't leave me alone!"

Bannon said slowly, "I must say I have the same impression of him, though I ain't in a position to criticize him or any other man. Kit—" She turned toward him quickly, at something in the way he said her name. But that was all. If she expected more, it didn't come. He turned abruptly and started for the corral, leading the now-docile stud.

Chapter 12

The man with the scar arrived in Mitchell during the hour before noon on Friday to find Main Street without life or activity, in midday stillness. He took his time, studying out the straggle of buildings along the creek as a sturdy gray gelding carried him down the canyon. The man was tall, rangily built, and, like the horse, looked as though he had traveled a considerable distance.

He wasn't showing a gun, though there could always be one in a pocket of his saddlebags or under his canvas jacket.

As he neared the foot of the street, Howie Whipple was just crossing the work area in front of the livery stable with a load of harness slung across one bony shoulder. It was probably the sight of the first human being he'd encountered here that caused the stranger to draw rein, calling out as he kneed the gray over. Howie turned and looked up and halted in his tracks.

Old scar tissue shining faintly against a sun-browned and shaven cheek, the stranger returned Howie's look and asked, "What's this town called?"

The towheaded hostler seemed to have trouble getting his tongue to work. "Mitchell," he said finally.

"Named for somebody, of course?"

"I dunno. I never heard."

The stranger considered Howie Whipple as though trying to fathom what was eating at him; he appeared to give it up and his thin mouth twisted. "Well," he commented, with poorly concealed sarcasm, "you look like an intelligent young man. Perhaps you can answer a question or two for me. First of all, where in this town of yours would I be apt to buy a decent meal?"

He got no answer at all this time. Howie opened his mouth and then closed it again, while he continued to stare at the stranger in a way that suggested something had knocked all the words out of his head. The stranger's face darkened and he frowned, with the beginnings of impatience; but at that moment he glimpsed the girl who had appeared in the barn doorway. He turned to look at her as she said, "Is there anything wrong, Howie?"

Before the towhead could answer, the man on the gray said irritably, "Is this fellow simple or what? I asked him a plain question about your local restaurants. I can't get anything out of him."

"Restaurants?" Kit Tracy came forward. Her gaze, like Howie Whipple's, seemed pinned to the stranger's face. She had to draw a breath and make an effort to put her mind on an answer. "The one up the street is all right, I guess. They serve meals at the hotel, too."

"I see. Thank you." Having learned what he wanted, the stranger continued to look at her with bold admiration. Howie Whipple had started for the barn now with his shoulderload of harness, but he continued to look back, half stumbling once as he failed to put his mind on where his feet were going.

The stranger demanded suddenly, "Do you people

think you know me from somewhere? Frank Conger is the name. I've never seen this town before today—but the way you both act, I could almost believe you were *expecting* me!"

She made almost a startled movement with one hand. "Oh, no—of course not!" Her cheeks reddened slightly, in confusion. "I'm sorry, Mr. Conger. I—I suppose we just don't see many strangers, back here."

The man on the gray shifted position and put up a hand to rub a thumb idly across his right cheek, where the scar, which looked as though it might actually have been an old bullet wound, lost itself in a full, tawny sideburn. It seemed to be an unconscious gesture.

He said suddenly, "I wonder. Would there happen to have been another loose rider besides me pass through here, within the last week most likely? He'd be a man not quite my size—black hair and moustache. Of course, he might have seen fit to get rid of that by now."

Kit Tracy swallowed. "You think he'd have come through Mitchell?"

"I'm close enough on his heels, I'm virtually certain of it. I see no way at all he could have lost me."

She showed him a face that was more like a mask, her thoughts concealed behind it. "The way you talk," she said, "the man sounds like some kind of criminal. Maybe you have a warrant for him?"

"I never said so, miss," Frank Conger reminded her. "I just asked if you'd seen him."

"I'm sorry," she said stiffly. "I can't help you." And she ended the conversation by turning and marching away from him into the barn and the partitioned corner that held her grandfather's office.

But there, the brisk resolution deserted her. She walked to the desk and dropped her hands onto the back of the chair, and suddenly her hands were trembling so that she had to clamp them tight to steady herself.

She was still standing like that, fighting for control, when a sound made her head jerk about. Her eyes widened as she saw the stranger had followed her and stood in the office doorway, arms folded, silently watching her. When she gasped and drew back a step, the man lifted a reassuring hand. "No need to be alarmed," he said. "I don't mean to trouble you."

"Then what *do* you want?" she demanded sharply, trying to cover the start of real fear.

The dark eyes that rested on her held a hint of mockery, telling her more clearly than words that he had seen through her, not been deceived or put off by her at all. He said now, "I think I'd better tell you that I'm a pretty determined fellow. What's more, this Ed Bannon I've been talking about—well, you might say that he has a way about him when he wants to. To be blunt, I'd hate to think I'd missed my chance at him, all because some pretty girl had romantic notions about lying to protect him. Believe me, she'd be using very poor judgment."

Anger overcame her bout of trembling. Coldly, she said, "I have no idea what you're talking about, but I don't think I'm interested."

"No?" He had a scornful look that seemed to probe behind a person's speech and peel away, almost with amusement, the layers of pretense. He merely looked at her now, for a long moment, before he said flatly, "Well, I'm glad to hear that. I wouldn't like to think you were interested in a man who'd run off with his boss's wife. Because that's what we're dealing with here. Yes, that's Ed Bannon," he went on. "The woman in question was married to a Montana horse rancher; Bannon was her husband's top wrangler and a damned good horseman. He could have been fixed in that job for life—but I guess pulling wages wasn't good enough for him.

"Anyway, the rancher has his wife back; now he wants Bannon and he wants him very bad. Which is the reason I'm here. You asked me, do I carry a warrant? No, miss. I'm not a lawman—but I've got a commission to bring back the man who cuckolded Virgil Hardman, and there's good money in it if I do. Hardman's got just about all the money in Montana."

Somehow, in answering, Kit managed to control her voice, to maintain the icy calm she hoped would disguise her real emotions. "All I know is, I think you've come to the wrong place if you hope to collect it!"

"If you say so." Frank Conger seemed willing to let it go at that. He straightened from his negligent lean against the side of the door. "You'll pardon me, I hope, for taking up your time. You said I could get a good meal up the street. I don't suppose you'd do me the honor of joining me?"

She shook her head. "No, thank you."

"No harm in asking." The man hunter accepted his dismissal with a faint hint of a smile which to her had a cruel and mocking edge. And then he turned and was gone, and she felt reaction wash over her.

Her eyes blurred with tears, but they were tears of anger. She shook her head, dashed the back of a hand across her eyes, got a handkerchief from a pocket of her skirt, and blew her nose forcefully. What he had told her could *not* be true! And yet . . .

She had to recognize that it fit the gaps in her knowledge. Bannon had told her very little, while this man's story had been circumstantial in explaining his skill with horses and his reticence in revealing anything much about himself.

Naturally, Ed Bannon wouldn't mention an affair with another man's wife!

But all such thoughts were suddenly irrelevant. There was something that needed to be done, and it sent her hurrying through the stable. As she stepped outside Howie Whipple came up, his face working with excitement.

"Kit!" he exclaimed. "That *was* the man, wasn't it—the one I'm supposed to be lookin' out for? By dog, I'm almost sure!"

She interrupted impatiently. "Listen to me, Howie! We've got to find Mr. Bannon and tell him—and we've got to do it *fast!* He could be almost any place. At the jail. Or maybe at Doc Ashby's having a visit with Sam . . ."

The towhead was frowning in concentration, peering along the sun-filled street. "I don't reckon he's either of them places, Kit. Because don't I see that dun horse of his, tied right there in front of the restaurant?"

"What!" Almost afraid to, she turned and looked and saw the dun—and the man hunter already dismounting to place his gelding alongside it. "Oh, Howie!" she moaned. "We're too late!" Heart knocking against her ribs, she could only stand helplessly watching as Frank Conger ducked beneath the rail and walked inside the eating place.

There was a counter with stools along it, a couple of tables next to the window that were spread with red-checked cloths, other tables against the side walls. A piece of slate above the counter held the day's menu, written in chalk; steamy smells of cooking issued from beyond the curtained door into the kitchen. It was still early for the regular dinner business, however. A single customer was seated at a corner table, a serving of meat loaf and green beans and stewed tomatoes before him.

He was just setting a coffee cup into its saucer as the newcomer paused in the doorway, and Conger and Ed Bannon looked at one another across the still and empty restaurant. Neither allowed more than the briefest look of surprise to alter the careful set of his features.

Frank Conger left the door then and walked past unoccupied stools and tables to the place where Bannon sat alone. He put a hand on the chair opposite and said without expression, "This place taken?"

"Doesn't appear to be."

It was all the invitation Conger needed. He sat, took off his hat with its sweat-stained band, and dropped it on the floor beside his chair. Bannon calmly continued eating. Conger, straightening, went suddenly still as he saw a gleam of metal on the other's shirt beneath his coat. For once, a reaction was startled from him.

"By God, I don't believe it! Is that thing real?"

"You can believe it, Conger," Bannon told him calmly. "I'm not sure you'd believe how I came to wear a town marshal's badge, but that's beside the point. It doesn't really concern you."

"It doesn't make any sense!" Frank Conger exclaimed. "Just how long can you have been in this town?"

"A few days—since Sunday. I wouldn't advise trying to figure it out."

A man wearing an apron and a striped shirt with rolled-up sleeves brought a glass of water and fistful of silverware, which he dumped in front of his new customer. He asked, "What can I do for you?"

Conger looked at Bannon's plate. "How's the meat loaf?"

"I've eaten worse."

"Bring me the same." The man went back to his kitchen, leaving them alone again. Bannon went on with his eating, seemingly unconcerned. Frank Conger said heavily, "All right, so we'll forget the badge. I suppose you know you've been leading me quite a chase."

"I hope Virg Hardman's paying enough to make it worth your trouble."

"Don't worry . . . What I'm curious to know is, just how long you've been aware I was on your trail?"

Bannon took another drag at his coffee cup. "I assumed somebody would be. I didn't know it was you, until that night I sighted you in Boise."

"You almost lost me there for good," the other man admitted. "I thought you'd headed south."

"It's what you were supposed to think. Too bad you didn't stay fooled."

Conger said, "I certainly never expected you to stop here, of all places, and let me catch up with you!"

He broke off then, as the restaurant man came with his food and a pot of coffee. While the cup was being filled, the restaurant door suddenly opened and Kit Tracy burst in.

She halted abruptly, wide-eyed, as though unable

to believe the sight of these two men calmly seated with food on the table between them. She came forward a few steps, nearly stumbling, and blindly let herself on to a chair at one of the tables. When the restaurant man stopped beside her she shook her head, not looking at him, and sent him away grumbling, without an order.

Frank Conger had noticed her. He halted a fork on its way to his mouth and looked over at her pale face and distraught expression. He nodded. "Well, well! The young lady from the stable! I'm not surprised to know she was lying. I figured, Bannon, you had a way with women; you seem to have a good eye for them, too."

For the first time Ed Bannon showed a reaction. He looked at Kit and again, sharply, at the man hunter. "You talked to her? How much did you say?"

"Enough, I'd have thought, to jar loose some of the truth. Yet she still wouldn't admit she'd ever seen you—or that you'd put her on the lookout for whenever I arrived."

He had broken through the other man's composure, no doubt of it now. Ed Bannon's jaw muscles were bunched hard. "You'll do anything, or use anyone!"

"That's the kind of game I'm in," Frank Conger said. "I play for keeps. Now you'd better finish your meal. As soon as we're done here, we'll be riding."

He returned to his own feeding. He was a smooth and efficient eater, who went at his meal with full concentration on emptying the plate. Ed Bannon, for his part, seemed to have lost all taste for his dinner. He looked at what was left of it and with a flat grimace dropped his fork into the plate and pushed it away from him. Conger observed this with a faint smile, as though it amused him.

Two townsmen entered and noisily took places at a table by the window, talking loudly as they went through the routine of making their choices from the chalked-up menu. Kit Tracy had hardly moved, where she sat alone with her white-knuckled hands tightly clasped and her intent stare on Bannon and the man hunter. The proprietor came and took orders from his new customers and ducked back through the kitchen partition.

Frank Conger had finished cleaning his plate. When both men had put down money in payment for their meals, Ed Bannon suggested in a strange, flat tone, "Pick up your hat—and while you're about it, have a look under the table."

Conger gave him a probing look that tried to read a meaning behind the words. After a frozen moment, he leaned deliberately for the dusty head-gear beside his boot; that way, he was able to see beneath the edge of the red-checked cloth and into the black muzzle of a gun in Bannon's left hand, where it rested on his knee. Conger jerked upright. Bannon said in the same tone, meant only for his ears, "That's right, friend. It's been there and ready ever since I caught sight of you through the window, tying up your horse. Now," he ordered, "you get on your feet and we'll walk out of here—casual and friendly."

Without moving, the other man said coldly, "And suppose I refuse? You're not going to gutshoot me, in front of witnesses—certainly not in front of the girl!"

"No, but I can nail you in an ankle. The shooting

would look like an accident, and it would cripple you—long enough, at least, for me to get out of here. You see, I can play for keeps myself when I have to!" He motioned with his head. "Up!" But immediately he corrected himself: "No—wait. First—very carefully and using both hands—open the front of that coat."

The man hunter's cold eyes flickered with chagrin, but Bannon's threat was enough to make him spread the canvas jacket. Bannon reached across the littered table and quickly lifted the snub-nosed revolver from its holster under the man's left arm; he dropped it into a pocket of his own coat, making certain the action was observed by no one except, perhaps, Kit Tracy. That done, he switched his own six-shooter to his right hand and slid it into its holster. Keeping his hand on it he told Conger, "All right. We'll be going, now . . ."

There was no resistance; Conger appeared to be persuaded. They rose together and Bannon motioned the other ahead of him. The restaurant man, returning from the kitchen with steaming plates in both hands, called a cheery, "See you again, gentlemen," to which Bannon merely nodded. After that they were on their way to the door, and as they passed her table Bannon gave Kit Tracy a glance into which he tried to put some kind of reassurance.

Outside, they untied their horses and, almost in one movement, swung astride. Conger waited for instructions, got a nod of Bannon's head downcanyon. As they started along the street, with Bannon holding a half length to the rear where he could keep a watch on his prisoner, Kit Tracy came hurrying from the restaurant. She placed both trembling hands on the weathered hitching rail and leaned her weight on them, while she anxiously watched the two riders move away from her.

The two rode without haste down the twisting street, keeping to a slow walk, each man warily conscious of the other. Their horses splashed through the shallow fording of the creek and passed the few last straggling buildings of the town, and now Ed Bannon broke the silence to say, "Maybe I can ask you to tell me one thing: Lucy Hardman—she did manage to get away?"

The question made Conger turn his head and favor Bannon with a long and searching look. " 'Manage'?" he repeated. "Maybe you had better chew that one a little finer."

"Hardman's men nearly overtook us that night," Bannon explained a shade impatiently. "There wasn't time to make sure of the finish. I had to leave his wife waiting at that siding for the train that would have been coming through, inside another hour. I took the horses and led the pursuit away, so that she would have her chance to stop the train and board it. I never saw her again—there was no way I could find out what happened."

Something seemed to amuse the other man. The thin lips quirked faintly and Frank Conger said, "Then I can put you straight. Mrs. Hardman never left at all! She must have thought better of it, because next day she went back to her husband and made up with him. She explained that the whole thing had been your doing and your idea. She told him you had her fooled for awhile, before she realized all you were really after was a way to get money out of her husband."

Ed Bannon's face was a tight mask. "You're telling me Hardman believed her?"

"Eventually—though I guess he gave her a bad time at first. But he saved the worst for *you*. That's when he put out the call for you—but not dead or alive. You're no use to him dead. He wants you delivered to him whole, so he can strip the hide off you himself!"

"That sounds like Virg Hardman," Bannon agreed bleakly and let the subject drop.

They were out of the town, now, and the canyon walls had leveled off and rock-ribbed hills sent back the brilliant sunlight. Abruptly Bannon reined to a halt, drawing his gun, and Conger pulled his horse around and they faced each other in the noontime stillness. Conger said, with an edge of strain showing in the harshness of his voice, "I suppose this is where you put a bullet in me and throw my body in the creek!"

The stream flowed swiftly here in its rocky bed, sucking at the rank growth in the shallows, glittering in the sun. Bannon looked at the water, as if he half considered the suggestion, but then he looked again at the prisoner and shook his head. "I suppose I'll be sorry I didn't," he admitted grimly. "I don't really know what to do with you; so I suppose the answer is—nothing."

The man hunter's eyes narrowed. "You mean to let me go?" he demanded, and he warned, "I'm not a man that quits, Bannon. I certainly didn't ride this far for nothing."

"I never thought you had. One thing I'm not fool enough to do," Bannon said, "is turn my back on you before I make sure you haven't got another gun on you somewhere. So, lift your hands and sit tight—and don't try anything while I'm finding out."

With the gun leveled between them and the prisoner's arms raised, Bannon kneed his dun closer where he could check the saddlebags slung across the gray's withers. They held personal possessions, mostly innocuous, though in one he found a box of cartridges for the captured gun. Bannon took this, dropped it into a pocket of his coat. He even examined the rolled blankets, tied with Conger's slicker behind the cantle.

Satisfied, he backed away and slid his own gun back into the holster. "You're clean, I guess," he said. "You can go."

Conger said bluntly, "You're a fool! Perhaps you think I can't get hold of another revolver. Hell, this country's full of them!"

"I'm sure you can—and I don't doubt you'll be back. But here's a thought for you to chew on: you said yourself I wouldn't be worth anything to Virg Hardman except alive and on the hoof. So you can't afford to kill me—but for my part, I'm a pretty desperate man. I'll kill *you* before I let myself be dragged off to Montana. That's a promise, Conger, and it may make the job a little tougher than you had figured. Think it over."

"And while I'm doing that," the man hunter suggested dryly, "I suppose you'll be sneaking out on me again. I'll just have to hunt you down a second time."

Bannon replied, "That's *your* problem. I have my own. I've taken on a job here; I won't be leaving till it's finished."

For a moment each of these men considered the other, trying to take his measure or locate some source of weakness—and not finding one. There seemed no more value in words. Abruptly, Ed Bannon reined the dun about and lifted into a lope as he headed back down the wagon road, toward the village in the canyon.

Chapter 13

The third time Kit Tracy multiplied seven times eight and got sixty-four, she gave it up and laid her pen down and dropped her head into her hands. Her thoughts were in no shape for wrestling with accounts receivable; the hard knot of coldness at the pit of her stomach was a physical thing that sapped her powers of concentration.

The name for this emotion, of course, was fear: fear and worry for Ed Bannon, which deepened as the half hour passed since she had watched him and the man named Conger leaving the restaurant together. True enough, she had seen Bannon disarm his enemy, and she had no doubt that Bannon knew how to take care of himself. But she was thoroughly aware that, even without a gun, Frank Conger was a dangerous man. Though she hadn't been able to hear a word of the quiet talk that passed between them there at the table in the restaurant, she had felt the strong undercurrents. And now she had the uncertainty of not knowing what was happening— where the two had ridden together, or whether in fact she would ever know.

It was that thought which, more than once in this half hour, had brought her to her feet and nearly sent her out of the office, to throw the saddle on her little mare and take off after them. But each time something stopped her. She had sense enough to know that even if she caught up with them, she would have been powerless to interfere with two such determined men. Yet it was something more that held her back—the appalling things Conger had said to her concerning Ed Bannon, things she didn't want to believe but which somehow, as Conger told them, held a somber ring of truth. They altered the image she'd allowed herself to form of Ed Bannon, gave her such a disquieting new perspective that all at once she no longer knew what she thought about him. And indecision held her where she was.

But now an angry restlessness seized her. Suddenly she could sit still no longer, and she struck both fists against the arms of her chair and leaped to her feet. In a sudden feverish need for action she hurried out into the barn, calling for Howie so that she could tell him she would be leaving him in charge of the stable for an hour or two. She got her saddle off the rack, toted it into Ginger's stall. She had the blanket in place and smoothed out and was reaching to lift on the saddle, when she heard footsteps approaching through the straw-littered aisle between the stalls.

She turned, saying, "Howie, I want you to—" And broke off as she saw it wasn't the hostler's string-bean silhouette, shaping up against the bright sunglare beyond the doorway.

Ed Bannon told her, "No. It's not Howie . . ."

She looked past him, seeing the dun standing on trailing reins just outside the door. Quickly she demanded, "What became of—?"

"He's gone. For the time being, anyway."

"Then he isn't—? You didn't—?"

"Kill him? You thought that was what I had in mind?" He shook his head. "No, I didn't kill him. He's going to be around, out there somewhere— looking for his chance. One thing it means, I guess, is no more sessions at that corral with the black."

When she made no answer to that he went on, in a note of urgency, "Kit, I have to talk to you—if you're still willing."

She almost refused, but then she said, "Wait for me in the office." Prey to a jumble of emotions, but mostly sheer physical relief at seeing he seemed to have survived whatever transpired with Frank Conger, she stood and watched him walk away from her. Afterward she replaced her saddle on the rack where it belonged and folded and hung up the blanket.

When, moments later, she entered the office, it was to find Bannon slumped in the chair by the desk, his hat on the floor beside him, legs stretched out and head back, his eyes closed. She looked at him a long moment, thinking in that moment he looked completely vulnerable, unguarded, marked by clear signs of the ordeal he had just been through. When she closed the door he opened his eyes and sat straighter in his chair as she came and took her own place at the desk.

"What happened with Conger?" she demanded.

"Not a great deal," Bannon said. "I'd already taken his gun, and there wasn't much just then he could do; but I'm sure he isn't through with me. Kit . . ." He breathed deeply and ran the palm of a hand down across his face. It seemed difficult for him to continue. "Conger had a talk with you—I found out that much. He told you some things about me."

She was looking at her hands, folded in front of

her on the desk. "He did," she admitted in a small voice. "About a woman in Montana."

"Another man's wife." Bannon nodded, and the muscles along his jaw were hard. "It isn't hard to imagine what you must think of me now! To come riding in here the way I did—with *that* behind me—and never let on, never give you a hint of the truth . . ."

"You didn't owe me anything."

He slapped a hand upon the desk. "Kit, I don't *want* you thinking things like that about me! Because, whatever you heard, you didn't hear all of it. I do have my side of the story—if you'll listen."

"But of course I'll listen," Kit said quickly. "Why should I take only the word of a total stranger like Frank Conger, who was probably lying anyway?"

"No. He wasn't lying," Bannon said, shaking his head. "By his own lights, Conger's an honest man. I can't doubt that what he told you was facts, as far as he knew them. Trouble is, I don't quite know how I'm going to tell you the rest without seeming to do something I don't want to, by putting the blame on somebody else—especially a woman. I keep telling myself she must have been desperate, or at least thought she was, to do what she did. Besides, you could say I was plenty old enough to know better."

Kit told him gravely, "You're beginning to talk in circles. Suppose you just tell me?"

"All right. I'll make it as short as I can . . . Lucy Hardman was—still is—a very handsome woman, married to a man rich enough to have bought this John Luft of yours several times over; the horse ranch that I ran for him was only one of many enterprises. The ranch was a long way from anyplace, with a rough crew, but that's where he kept her even when he was gone himself—maybe for weeks at a time. I know she must have hated it there, something like you tell me *you* would feel being stuck at the JL, alone with men such as Reub Springer.

"From the day I started to work I could see how unhappy she was, and I couldn't really blame her. Virg Hardman ain't what you'd call a lovable man. I figured it must have been mostly his bankroll she'd married, and if it was, she hadn't got much good out of it. Oh, she owned a wardrobe full of nice clothes that she liked to dress up in, but there was no place to wear them except that drafty log barn of a house—not another woman in sight, except for a Crow Indian housekeeper. At first, when I saw how things stood, she struck me as sort of pathetic."

"Only at first?" Kit Tracy asked.

"After that, I got resentful," he said. "Hardman had a mean streak, which he took out sometimes on the men who worked for him. And that was all right—it's part of what we were paid for. But it bothered me to see his meanness show up in his relations with his wife. She must have guessed how I felt because she began coming to me with her troubles; I was really the only person she had to talk to. Finally, one day when he left after a really bad row, her face was bruised and her eye was swollen and she begged me to help her get away before he could beat her up again. She said she'd go anywhere with me, do anything . . ."

Under the weight of Kit's steady, listening gaze, Ed Bannon looked suddenly uncomfortable. He shifted in his chair and his broad cheeks colored. "All right!" he said gruffly. "So I should have known better. By that time I figured I was more than half in love with her. Believe me," he exclaimed, "I ain't proud of any part of what I'm telling you!"

Kit said quietly, coldly, "Go on. You gave up your job?"

"Oh, I was ready to anyhow—I'd had more than enough of Virg Hardman, *and* his job. I saddled us a couple of horses and we lit out. We traveled light— she took hardly any of the stuff Hardman had given her. But from the start, nothing went right. Somebody saw us leave, and they got on the telephone and notified Hardman, and in no time he had a small army out, looking to head us off . . ."

She stared at him, scarcely breathing, as he related in the baldest terms the ordeal of their escape—of how, finally, he had left Lucy Hardman standing beside a flag stop on the Northern Pacific while he took both horses and rode away, to lay a false spoor and draw the pursuers from her. "That was the end of it," he said. "It was two months ago, and ever since I've been on the run."

Frowning, Kit prompted him, "You never saw the woman again? Haven't you even tried?" When he shook his head she exclaimed, "But I don't understand. If you were in love with her . . ."

"I wasn't, by that time. Everything had changed while we were running away from her husband's men. The whole thing became my fault—she used language on me I'd never heard from any woman! Of course, I knew she was frightened and upset, but just the same, she said enough to make it clear she'd always looked on me as a dupe and a fool— someone who could be used.

"And what I've found out today makes it even clearer," Bannon went on in the same flat tone.

"Frank Conger tells me she never took the train. She must have thought it all over and realized what she'd be giving up when she left Virg Hardman. Anyway, she went back and made it up with him. She lied and laid all the blame on me—and that's when Frank Conger was hired to pick up my trail and take me back for Hardman to settle with . . ." Ed Bannon ended gruffly, "Well, that's the story. I told you I wasn't proud of any of it."

"No," Kit said slowly, staring at him. "I shouldn't think you would be! This woman," she went on with an effort, past the heavy lump that seemed to have formed in her chest. "You accuse her of heaping all the blame on you. But where is that any different from what you're doing now?"

He looked as though she had struck him. His head jerked up and his dark face drained of some of its color. It seemed to be a moment before he could form words. "Is that how you see it? You think I've been lying to you, I guess—trying to make myself look better, by shifting the guilt to Lucy Hardman. Just because she isn't here to defend herself . . ."

"I don't know what to believe!" Kit Tracy cried and burst into tears.

She dropped her head onto her forearms, fighting the sobs that tore her apart. At first there was nothing from Bannon. Then the timbers of his chair creaked as he rose to his feet, and his footsteps crossed to the door. Pausing there he spoke, in a muffled voice, "I wish there was something useful I could say, but I guess there isn't."

He seemed to be waiting for some answer, but when she neither spoke nor raised her head to look at him, he said then, in a tone devoid of emotion, "Very well . . . About the black—I'm sorry we didn't get to finish working with him. But he's coming along. Just go on being gentle with him, and I know you'll be riding him in no time at all . . . Goodbye, Kit."

There was the sound of the door opening, and Ed Bannon was gone.

Ashby's waiting room was empty. Bannon called out and, getting no answer, went on through into the other room where Sam Prentiss lay. At first glance Sam did not look nearly so well as he had yesterday; the marshal's face, in the shadow of the drawn window shade, wore an alarming pallor, and the eyes in the seamed face showed no flicker of recognition. But Bannon was full of his own problems. He advanced into the room and began without preliminaries: "Sam, I'm afraid I've got bad news for you. I won't go into long explanations. It's just that the trouble we both knew I was expecting has finally caught up with me."

He thought the lawman was going to speak; Sam's lips stirred but no words came out. Being himself in a hurry and anxious to have this over with, Ed Bannon plunged ahead: "I'm sorry. I know I promised to stay until you were on your feet again, though I guess you must have realized that was a promise I might not be able to keep. Well, I'm afraid now you'll have to manage without me."

He waited for a reaction. Sam Prentiss still had no answer. His head remained motionless on the pillow, his hands lay upon the counterpane. And now as Bannon watched, with a sudden stirring of alarm, he saw the fixed gaze waver and then move on, leaving him, to drift over toward the window.

"Sam?"

D. B. Newton

Bannon started to move closer to the bed and at that moment heard Doc Ashby's step. The doctor, entering, shouldered brusquely past and bent for a close look at his patient.

Bannon exclaimed, "He's worse again, isn't he? What went wrong?"

"It was his own dumb fault," the doctor said. "I told him not to get out of bed without me being there—I was sure he must be a lot weaker than he thought, after all this time flat on his back. But of course, he wouldn't listen. This morning he tried it and had a fall and tore out a couple of stitches. It's set him back."

"Why does he look like this?"

"He's under sedation. He was so furious, I had to give him something to calm him down—afraid he'd hurt himself worse. It may be a couple more hours," Ashby went on, "before his head clears up enough that you can talk to him. Any message you want to leave?"

Ed Bannon considered, looking at the waxen face of the hurt man. Something seemed to settle in him then; the urgency that had been in him a moment ago was put aside. He drew a breath. "No," he said slowly. "No, I guess not. Just tell him not to rush things—take whatever time he needs."

"That's the best advice anyone can give," the doctor agreed. "But Sam Prentiss is hardly the man to take it . . ."

As they went back into the waiting room at the front of the house, the doctor was saying, "I guess I didn't hear you, when you came up just now. I was out back, getting in some fruit. Here . . ." He picked up a bowl of tree-ripened plums. "Help yourself. They taste pretty good."

"Thanks."

Bannon took several, slipping them into a pocket of his coat. As he left the doctor's house he found himself in a mood of restless frustration—having made up his mind he could no longer stay in the same town with Kit Tracy, only to be thwarted by Sam Prentiss' turn for the worse. Under the spur of it, instead of climbing the hill to the gloomy jailhouse, he crossed the street and walked out onto the picnic ground.

He found it deserted except for a solitary figure seated on a table near the creek. Bannon looked at the dejected lines of the man's shoulders and saw that it was Bert Maroon. The young fellow looked up as he approached.

"Oh—hello, Mr. Bannon."

Bannon nodded and took a perch beside him on the table's edge. For a moment neither spoke. The creek burbled at their feet, the bare slope rising beyond in the late sunlight. "Have a plum?" Bannon suggested. Maroon shook his head, and Bannon set to work on it himself while the silence deepened. Finally he asked bluntly, "What's bothering you?"

Bert Maroon shrugged. "Nothing much, I guess."

"It doesn't seem like nothing. You look like the bottom had dropped out." Bannon tossed the plum seed into the creek, sucked juice from his fingers. "Wouldn't have anything to do with Miss Weiker?"

At that the other man's head jerked up, his eyes met Bannon's. "What makes you think—?" The spirit ran out of him and he said, morosely, "Is it plain as all that?"

"Oh, I don't know. It's just that the other day, here at the picnic, I couldn't help but notice you didn't seem to be enjoying yourself very much."

"What is it with women, Mr. Bannon?" the younger man exclaimed, suddenly driven to let out the thing that was gnawing inside him. "Why is she like that; one minute nice as can be and then the next . . . D'you think it's because I'm just a nobody, who works in her pa's store? Is that why she hasn't any real use for me? You been around, Mr. Bannon—what do *you* think?"

Thinking just then of Kit Tracy and of Lucy Hardman, Bannon was struck with the irony of being asked for advice in a matter he found as bewildering as it could possibly be to Bert Maroon. He shook his head. "Getting around doesn't always make that much difference where women are concerned, Bert," he commented. "Doesn't matter who you are—sometimes they can have you crossed up so bad, there finally doesn't seem anything to do but simply pick up and leave!"

"Leave?" the young fellow echoed. He shook his head. "But that means leaving Mitchell, and I'd hate to do that. I've knocked around some; I like this town, better'n any I ever seen. Still, if you have to go on seeing somebody, everywhere you turn—knowing you ain't got a chance with her—that's no good, either!"

"You're right—it isn't," Bannon agreed heavily. "But a man can find he's run out of good choices!"

They watched the flowing of the creek after that in silence.

Chapter 14

Toward dusk on Saturday came the call for help from Wilcey Chipman. The messenger he sent found Bannon talking with the mayor, on the front steps of Weiker's Emporium. The man said, "I was told to find you, quick! It's Reub Springer. The boss thinks he's out for trouble."

"All right."

Bannon and the mayor exchanged a bleak look. Saturday—the one night when every little town across the cattle ranges, lying half asleep and empty through the working week, drew its ration of ranch crews with thirsts to quench and hours of monotonous labor to forget . . . Early as it was, Mitchell already echoed to the sound of horsemen arriving, of spurs ringing on the sidewalks, of rough male voices. The JL was sure to be sending in its contingent; Bannon hadn't been aware they'd already arrived. But if Reub Springer was among them it was a good bet his expulsion from Monday's picnic would still be rankling. It was all the excuse he would need to make trouble for somebody.

"I'll just walk up there with you," Jess Weiker said heavily. "Do no harm to remind him again you've got the town's backing. Wait a second while I speak to Bert." He opened the door and called in to tell Bert Maroon he would be in charge of things. Afterward,

Bannon and the mayor dropped down the porch steps, and started along the darkening street angling toward the lighted front of Chipman's.

Weiker was going on about something but Ed Bannon scarcely heard, giving his attention instead to probing darker shadows along the street and studying the half-seen shapes that crossed the squares of streaking window light. He was thinking about Frank Conger. There was no chance Conger had given up—in these past thirty hours he'd have had time enough to promote himself another gun and to determine on a way to accomplish what he had come here to do. Nor, with so many outsiders in town, was there a hope of checking on them all. Any one of these figures, moving half-seen in the early dark, might actually be Bannon's personal nemesis, waiting for an opportunity.

It was a nagging worry, to add to his troubled concern over Kit Tracy whom he'd been religiously avoiding since yesterday in the stable office. Kit and Virg Hardman's gunman were alike in never being far now from the demanding surface of his thoughts . . .

The moment he opened the door and stepped inside the saloon, Bannon knew why he had been summoned. Reub Springer was here, all right, with his usual crowd of friends—including Nick Garvey, who had been making himself scarce around town since the night of the Fourth of July. Garvey, at least—and Jeff Pitts and Harry Ruser—seemed to have learned a lesson from their previous encounters with Mitchell's acting marshal: none of the three was wearing a gun this evening. But Springer's was belted prominently and almost defiantly about his middle, as though he were waiting for somebody to try and take it away from him.

He and his cronies had taken over one of the pool tables at the rear of the room, where they were having a loud and quarrelsome time and threatening to drown out Wilcey Chipman's more orderly guests. Chipman wore a harassed look as he came forward to greet Bannon and the mayor. Just then Springer gave one of the other players a shove that nearly sent him sprawling, and in a burst of obscenities the man came back at him with a pool cue brandished threateningly. Chipman had to raise his voice against the uproar as he demanded, "Did you see that? If they start fighting amongst themselves, they could wreck this place!"

Ed Bannon might have pointed out, *They couldn't if you had a bouncer on the payroll who was tough enough to handle them.* Instead, he merely nodded, signed for Jess Weiker to stay back, and himself went down the long room toward the pool table, where tobacco smoke swirled in a cloud in the cone of light beneath the shaded overhead lamp.

He was almost upon them before any of the men there appeared to notice. It was Nick Garvey who suddenly caught a glimpse of him. Bannon saw his head jerk, and then he said something from the side of his mouth. Reub Springer turned, dropping his cue stick so hastily that it struck the table rim and fell clattering to the floor.

"So it's you!" Springer exclaimed, so explosively that his voice carried over every other sound. "You think you want something?"

Bannon came on to stop a couple of yards from the big man; he met Springer's stare coolly. "There's a complaint that you and your friends are getting out of hand. It seems a little early in the evening for that."

The massive jaw thrust belligerently. Into the stillness that was beginning to spread through the room Springer said, with rankling anger, "Mister, maybe you'd like to go to hell!"

"I'm doing a job," Bannon spoke quietly. "Let's get something clear, Springer. You've chosen to hold a grudge against me from the first hour I hit this town. But frankly I don't really care what you think of me, so long as you behave yourself."

"I'll do any damn thing I like!"

"You say that," Bannon said, "because with Sam Prentiss laid up—from a bullet *you* put in him—you think the town has to stand for it. But the town doesn't! I'm putting you on notice, right now. Behave yourself, if you don't want to be ordered out of Mitchell for the second time in one week!"

"By you?" The big man let a sneer lift his lip. "That I'd like to see!"

"Keep on the way you're going and I'll oblige you. But you won't get another warning!"

Reub Springer's thick chest swelled. He flung out a hand as he glared about him at the silenced crowd. "You all hear that? By God, what kind of a town is it that'll pick up some saddle tramp that drifts through, and pin a piece of metal on him and let him call himself the law?"

"You're going too far, Reub Springer!" That was Mayor Weiker, his face turned crimson. "Don't try telling us how we're to run our town!"

"Oh! So the mayor's sticking his oar in!"

It was said with a sneer that stung Weiker to genuine anger. "Yes! That's exactly what I'm doing!

Springer, the town expects you to keep the peace. And to make sure of it, I'm ordering you to hand over that gun. The acting marshal here will take it."

"The hell he will!"

What had been an exchange of angry words had suddenly become something more, as Reub Springer quickly dropped his hand to gun butt in defiance of any attempt to disarm him. It was a turn Bannon hadn't been looking for. Inwardly, he swore a little at Weiker for the reckless way he had aggravated matters, but there was nothing to be done about it now. He said, "You heard the mayor." And he came on a step, a hand extended for the weapon.

He half expected Springer to draw on him. The impulse was clearly there; Reub Springer's shoulders had settled a little and he was breathing quickly and shallowly through his mouth. But when Bannon took another step the range boss fell back, until halted by the high edge of the pool table. He stood like that and stared at the smaller man.

Perhaps it was the element of the unknown that held Springer—his not feeling yet he really had the measure of the one who confronted him. Or perhaps he wasn't quite so sure of himself with guns as he was when he had fists and brute strength going for him. His mouth worked furiously, but slowly the big hand lifted clear of the weapon.

Seeing that, Ed Bannon told him, "Now you're using your head!" His own hand rested on the butt of his holstered revolver. Without drawing it he said quietly, "Suppose you unbuckle that belt and lay the whole works there on the table . . ."

It cost Springer a visible effort, but he did as he was told and then moved aside, so that Bannon could step in and take belt and holster and gun.

"I'm piling up quite a collection of these at the jail," Bannon said, looking now at Garvey and Pitts and Ruser. "You boys are still welcome to get yours back. You know the terms."

Abruptly, without looking again at the baffled fury in Reub Springer's heavy features, he turned away carrying the captured weapon. Jess Weiker was waiting to say "Good work!" but Bannon only gave the mayor an angry look as he passed. He went on through the long room and outside, not pausing, and talk was beginning to build even as the door swung shut behind him.

He was walking away from the saloon when Jess Weiker came after him, calling, "Bannon! Wait!" He slowed then and let the storekeeper catch up. They stood there on the darkened sidewalk and Weiker demanded, "Is something bothering you?"

Bannon made no attempt to keep the fury out of his voice. "It's just that I don't like being pushed into a fight—and that's what could have happened. When you ordered me to take that gun off him, you had no way of knowing he'd give it up. He'd been drinking enough to be capable of anything."

Weiker was at once on the defensive. "The man needed taking down," he insisted. "If he'd been let keep his gun, he was bound to make real trouble before the evening was through. And I never had any doubt you could handle him."

"You didn't, eh? Thanks for your confidence!" Bannon said dryly. "Meanwhile, have you thought how you intend to handle John Luft? You know how he feels about anyone in Mitchell interfering with his crew. He's not going to approve of this, in any particular!"

Heading for the jail, Ed Bannon left the mayor

with that to think about. He wouldn't be surprised to learn that Jess Weiker lost a little sleep tonight over this turn in his relationship with his biggest customer. At the moment, Bannon wasn't in a mood to care.

Reub Springer had abandoned the pool table for serious drinking. He stood at Chipman's bar with his friends, knocking back drinks from the bar bottle and nursing a belligerent silence. Though few spoke to him directly, he had an angry conviction he was being secretly laughed at. As he brooded over what had been done to him tonight, he presently built up a head of steam that was past containing. Without warning he swore aloud, slapped an empty glass down on the wood, and, turning, bulled his way out of there.

Like the born followers they were, Nick Garvey and the other pair promptly left their drinks and went after him. They found him standing on the saloon steps. Garvey said, "Hey! What's on your mind, Reub?"

No need to be told what *they* were thinking. The three had come into town tonight for the specific purpose of watching Springer settle with Ed Bannon. Because of what they'd had to witness, their confidence was badly shaken; yet they were still hoping to see Reub Springer somehow put things right. He judged they would give him just about one chance.

Whiskey roughened his voice as he said now, "You guys stand back and watch. I'm going after that sonofabitch!"

"You mean Bannon?" Eagerness was in Garvey's question.

"Before the night's over I'm fixing him for good."

"You got no gun," he was reminded. "Even you can't do nothing against him without a gun."

Jeff Pitts said, "I can borrow you one, Reub. Let me nose around, it shouldn't be hard."

"No!" Springer was peering off down the street at the lighted facades of Mitchell's nighttime businesses. "I got a better idea. Damned if I ain't! Lifting my six-shooter was Jess Weiker's doing, wasn't it? Well, then he's gonna give me another!"

Like other places along Main Street, Weiker's Emporium had stayed open late to catch the Saturday night trade. But the store had nearly emptied and Bert Maroon was moving around, putting stuff away and getting ready to close. When Reub Springer kicked the door open and strode inside, the young fellow looked around in irritation that changed to something else when he got a good look at this late customer. Springer was weaving a little on his boots, his face flushed. The clerk asked with chilly politeness, "You wanted something?"

The big man had found what he was looking for. He walked over to the case that held a display of hunting knives and pistols. He laid both palms on the glass and said loudly, "This forty-four Smith & Wesson should do me. You can fetch me that. And a box of cartridges."

Young Maroon made no move to comply. "I don't think so."

"And why the hell not?"

"Mr. Weiker wouldn't allow it. I heard what happened this evening—him making you give your gun to the marshal . . ."

Reub Springer turned a menacing scowl on the store clerk. "You look, sonny! Jess Weiker ain't giving the orders now—*I* am. So, get over here and open this case."

"I've already told you—"

"Then I'll by God do it myself!"

He started around to where he could get at the sliding door. That brought an outcry from the boy: *"No!"* Bert Maroon sprang forward and laid hold of Springer to try and drag him away. And in fact the range boss was unsteady enough from the liquor he had consumed; despite his bulk he was thrown off balance.

Suddenly it was a struggle. They reeled through the narrow aisle between the counters. A rack holding a display of brooms went down with a clatter. From over at the street door Springer had left open, there was a sudden startled shout. Reub Springer paid no heed. He jerked free easily enough from his smaller opponent. He looked into Bert Maroon's sweating, frightened face and all his rage went into the contemptuous swipe of fist and forearm that struck the boy and sent him spinning.

Maroon's arms pinwheeled, his high-buttoned shoes tangled under him. Going down, he struck the edge of a counter, heavily, and fell on his back in the aisle. Reub Springer stood waiting with fists ready if he should try to get up and come at him again, but young Maroon lay motionless where he'd fallen. Springer cursed him and spat on the floor; then, satisfied there'd be no more trouble from that source, he remembered what he had come for and turned back to the case with the guns.

He didn't bother now with the sliding door. He simply put one heavy cowhide boot through the front, in a smash of exploding glass, and, reaching in, got the weapon he'd chosen, grunting as he cut himself on one of the jagged shards. He checked the cylinder, found it empty. But there were cardboard boxes of ammunition in the case also. Springer fished one out, fumbled it open, and began shoving cartridges into the chambers, too intent on what he was doing to heed a growing hubbub of voices beyond the open door.

Only as the last cartridge slid into its chamber did he become aware of someone striding toward him, broken glass crunching under solid boots. He turned and he saw the hated face of Ed Bannon, the glint of the metal badge on his coat, the gun in his hand. Springer, with a roar, slapped the cylinder home, swung up the loaded revolver, and fired.

The concussion of the shot beat against his eardrums, and through the film of powder smoke he saw his enemy still closing in on him, unhurt. Before he could work the trigger a second time Bannon struck his wrist and knocked it aside. In the next breath, a raised gun barrel reflected lamplight as it was swung, hard, against the side of Springer's skull. The light went out and Reub Springer dropped into pain and darkness.

The aftermath was confusion. Men tried to crowd into the store, for all Ed Bannon's efforts to keep them out and protect the pair of hurt men.

An eyewitness, tremulous and excited, kept telling anyone who would listen, "I saw it! I saw the whole thing. I heard shouting and I looked in, and there was Reub Springer trying to get the gun case open and the young fellow trying to stop him. I dunno where Bert Maroon ever got the nerve to stand up to anybody that size! The fight was over before it started. And Springer helped himself to a gun and, when the marshal came in, took a shot at him . . ."

Now the crowd split to make way for Doc Ashby, who had been summoned and arrived with Jess Weiker at his heels. Ashby only glanced at Reub Springer, sitting in a daze with knees pulled up and head on forearms.

Bannon said quickly, "I don't think Springer's bad hurt. I tapped him with a gun barrel, to keep from having to shoot him. But the boy don't look good to me."

Bert Maroon had not moved; he lay as still and pale as death as Ashby hurried to kneel beside him. They watched in silence as the doctor made his examination—feeling for a pulse, rolling back the boy's eyelids, and finally probing his skull with firm and careful fingers. Afterward he could only study the motionless features, his own expression grave, his lips pursed.

"Well?" Bannon demanded. "What is it?"

"I can't tell," Ashby said, getting to his feet. "A bad concussion, at the very least. He'll have to be watched close, to see what develops. Other than that, there's really nothing I know to do."

Jess Weiker exclaimed, "Do you mean he might *die?*"

"It's impossible to say. Springer must have knocked him hard enough against the edge of that counter to nearly smash a man's skull. I'll get a stretcher," he went on soberly. "We'll carry him over to my place. I'll have to set up a twenty-four-hour watch on him until I know, one way or the other."

Weiker was shaking in reaction to the thing that had happened here. He ran a hand across his cheeks and blurted, "No, Doc! That ain't right—you've got your hands full as it is. And the boy was hurt trying to protect my interests—it's my place to do whatever needs being done."

Bannon and the doctor both looked at him in surprise. It was Ashby who said, "You think you're up to it?"

The mayor seemed to have it settled in his own mind. "It's just as easy taking him up to my place as across the street. There'll be my wife, and Adeline, and me. And I'm sure others will help if we need it. No reason we can't keep a watch on him."

"All right." Ashby indeed looked as though a burden had been lifted from him. "I won't turn down an offer like that! You just be sure and let me know at once if there's any change. Get the word to me—any time at all! You understand?"

He gave Reub Springer a quick examination. At his touch the big man groggily lifted his head. There was blood in his hair where Bannon's gun barrel had broken the scalp, but Ashby said shortly, "Hell, he's all right—more drunk than anything else. Skull as thick as his, there's no call to worry. He'll come around."

Ashby hurried off, then, to arrange for a litter for Bert Maroon and the men to carry it. As Ed Bannon turned back from closing the door and shutting the curious crowd outside, he found Jess Weiker looking at the gun he'd picked up from the floor, still with the price tag hanging from it, and then helplessly at the wreckage of the smashed display case. Bannon said dryly, "I suppose Luft will make his usual generous offer to pay for the damages."

Weiker looked grim and unhappy. "Paying damages is the least of it this time. What do we do with *him?"* They both considered Reub Springer, seated in a scatter of broken glass and now beginning, vaguely, to show signs of awareness. "This isn't the same as busting up a barbecue!"

"No. It's assault and attempted robbery, for starters."

"And supposing—just supposing—Bert should die?" Jess Weiker's voice broke on the words.

"In that case, it's murder," Bannon replied. "Manslaughter, at the very least."

"But until we know—"

"Until then," Bannon finished, "this is one time when it's not enough just to set him on his horse and send him back to the JL. There can be only one place for him."

Weiker understood. He said bleakly, "John Luft isn't going to like this! He won't like it at all. But maybe he'll be able to see the sense of it."

"No difference. John Luft has had his way so long, he's spoiled. It has to stop sometime . . ." Bannon walked over to the big man and leaned to hook a firm hand under his arm.

"On your feet, Springer!" he ordered sharply. "You're going to jail."

Chapter 15

The church bell was sounding once more above the canyon, as it had that first morning when Ed Bannon rode in with the string of wild mustangs. It reminded him that this was Sunday again and, hard as it might be to realize it, he had now been here in Mitchell for only one short week.

He wasn't in the best of moods after a morning of listening to Reub Springer carrying on in his cell. Springer was suffering from a hangover and from a headache from the blow with Bannon's gun barrel. The fact that, after a more thorough examination, Doc Ashby had declared there was no real damage meant nothing to Reub Springer. He mixed complaints with obscenities and threats against Ed Bannon and the entire town of Mitchell for putting him where he was. When Bannon arranged for breakfast to be brought from the restaurant, for himself and for his prisoner, Springer declared it uneatable. Bannon refused to respond to his abuse; he pretended not even to hear, and after awhile the big man ran out of steam and, stretched out on his bunk, began to snore.

Bannon was straightening the office and sweeping out, listening to the church bell, and reflecting with mixed emotions on the events of this past week, when Jess Weiker walked in. The mayor said, "I just wanted to drop by for a moment before service and find how things are with you and your prisoner."

"The prisoner's fine," Bannon assured him, referring to the explosive sounds emanating from the barred cell. "Nothing wrong with his lungs, anyway. How's young Maroon?"

Weiker shook his head. "I wish I knew! So far there's no sign of him regaining consciousness. One or another of the family was by his bed, all night long. I'm real proud of Adeline," he added. "She's been a brick. She doesn't want anybody else doing anything for the boy—if she could she'd do it all herself."

Maybe she's growing up, Bannon thought.

"Just keep on as we're doing, Doc says—too early yet to tell anything." He slapped the desk, a restless gesture, and turned away. "I'd better go or I'll be late for service. Anything I can do for you here?"

"Nothing that I think of."

"All right. I'll keep in touch." Bannon nodded and watched the other man move toward the door. But there Weiker suddenly stiffened and exclaimed, "Hey, Bannon! Look at this!"

The acting marshal went quickly to join him. Weiker didn't need to point. It was John Luft, riding at a walk up the steep pitch of Nelson Street toward the jail. He came alone, this time without any entourage of his buckaroos. He sat a fine-looking bay, with the lines and the carriage indicative of good blood, and his stock saddle was worked with burnt-leather designs and flashed a gleam of silver trim. Weiker and Bannon stepped out to meet him and Luft reined in without dismounting. They looked at one another there in morning sunlight—the two townsmen bareheaded, the cowman with his solid features shaded under the wide brim of his hat.

Above them, on Piety Hill, the tolling of the bell had ceased; it left a stillness in its wake.

Luft piled his hands on the saddle horn and nodded toward the jail door. He said, "You've got my range boss locked up in there."

Ed Bannon acknowledged it. "You want to talk to him?"

"I want him turned loose!"

Bannon and the mayor exchanged a look. Jess Weiker, uneasy and troubled, said, "John, that isn't possible! Maybe you just haven't heard what he did last night."

Luft made an impatient gesture with one hard palm. "I heard all about it. I also heard he was drunk. When is this town going to learn about Reub Springer—that if you sell him likker, you're to blame if he does something stupid?"

"What he did last night," Bannon said, "was something a lot worse than stupid."

"So what of that? How much can the breakage on a glass case come to?"

"We're talking about a man's life."

"The clerk?" Luft shrugged. "I just now spoke to your Doc Ashby. He says there's a good chance the boy will be perfectly all right."

"I don't really think he said that," was Bannon's cold rejoinder. "According to what he's told us, there's just as good a chance Maroon won't make it. It's still touch and go."

The cowman didn't like being contradicted; his head lifted and angry color stung his craggy face.

He turned to Jess Weiker. "I'm not here to argue
with this so-called marshal of yours! I've got a cattle
ranch to run and I need my range boss—on the job,
not sitting in a jail. But I'll make you a deal: give me
Reub Springer, and then if it should come to the
worst for this clerk of yours, I'll see he's turned back
to you for trial. Now, tell me! Is there anything wrong
with that arrangement?"

Ed Bannon could see the mayor starting to waver.
Weiker said, "Do I have your word?"

"My solemn word," Luft assured him.

"And what are the chances of keeping it?" Ed
Bannon said curtly. "Once Springer is free, you can
bet he'll never let himself see the inside of this jail
again—least of all, to stand trial for murder! If Bert
Maroon dies, Springer will be gone for good, and
nothing anyone can do about it. Luft knows as
much," he told the mayor. "I think you do, too."

Hearing this, John Luft placed a long and stabbing look on Bannon. He told the mayor, "This man
of yours is damned insulting!"

Jess Weiker stared from one to the other. He was
an indecisive man, with responsibilities that were
probably beyond his powers to deal with. Bannon
could see he faced a hard decision. Unhappily the
mayor shook his head. "Maybe," he said slowly,
"he's only being practical . . ."

"*Practical!*" Anger pulled at Luft's mouth and
tightened it. "All right!" he snapped. "If it's practical
you want, then suppose you try figuring this—just
how much is the business I bring to that store worth
to you? How much would it cost you, and this thing
you call a town, if the JL was to suddenly stop coming here—ever? Remember, Weiker! It ain't so far

that I can't have whatever I need hauled out from Prineville or even down from The Dalles. Are you willing to pay that price?"

The storekeeper had turned white as the paint on the jail building. He tried to hold his voice steady but it trembled as he answered, "It's your privilege, I guess, to trade where you like!"

"Damn right it is!" John Luft stabbed a pointing finger. "So you think it over. I'll give you, and the town, twenty-four hours. If Reub Springer ain't out of that cell come noontime tomorrow—then I'll have to decide what measures I mean to take. It's entirely up to you!"

He had spoken louder, as his anger grew, and now there was a sudden cry from Reub Springer inside the jail: "Boss! Is that you? Goddammit, do something! Get me out of here!"

The rancher reined closer, the other two moving out of his way, and leaned slightly in the saddle to call through the open door: "Reub? Just take it easy. We'll get you out. And meanwhile, if they don't treat you right—they'll have me to answer!" Abruptly he straightened, the reins in his hands. He flicked a last, challenging look at the mayor and the acting marshal. "I've made myself clear," he said, and he pulled the bay around and kicked it into motion. It went cantering off down the steep side street and turned along the canyon, out of sight.

Left behind, Weiker and Bannon shared a look. Bannon eased out his breath and said roughly, "Well—I guess that's that."

"Twenty-four hours!" The mayor looked and sounded as though a weighty burden had been lowered onto his shoulders.

"And afterward? What do you think—if we *don't*

knuckle under and turn Springer over to him, will he really carry out his threat to boycott Mitchell? Or do you suppose he'd use force and try to *take* a prisoner out of this jail? Has even John Luft the arrogance for that?"

Jess Weiker spread both hands, an eloquent gesture. "Luft ain't a man that talks just to make a noise. He's set something afoot, and he'll have to follow it up—depend on that. I got to do some thinking," he added heavily and ran a palm across his jaw. "We—we'll talk about it later."

Abruptly he turned and walked on up the hill, and Ed Bannon watched him go—a troubled and shaken man, who might almost have aged a half dozen years during that scene with Luft.

That was the beginning.

With a prisoner in the cell, Ed Bannon found himself held more closely to the jail office than usual during the rest of a long day. Springer himself, taking his cue from that visit by his boss, had become more obnoxious than ever. He would not shut up. If he wasn't making demands—for food, drinking water, tobacco, or, if nothing else, to be taken to the outhouse in back of the jail—he spent his time taunting Bannon and making confident predictions: John Luft had promised his release in twenty-four hours; John Luft would do what he said. And once he was free, there were matters that needed settling between Springer and Bannon, and they would be taken care of.

The man didn't seem even to think of Bert Maroon, lying between life and death. It appeared no concern of his at all.

Springer, with his continual threats, wasn't the

only reminder of John Luft's promise. The word hadn't needed long to spread, and Bannon soon sensed that all Mitchell knew and took it seriously. As the afternoon wore on, men he scarcely knew took to dropping in at the office and to stopping him on the street when he went out for a brief tour of the town or simply to get away from Springer for a few minutes.

They were full of troubled questions. More than one expressed the opinion that Luft was no man to be satisfied with warnings and half measures—if he wanted his range boss freed, there were enough tough-handed men on the payroll that he might actually lead them here and take Reub Springer by force. And what would be Ed Bannon's response to that? What kind of action did he plan to take, and what did he expect from the town? These men were plainly worried; an air of anxious waiting seemed to be growing as the hours passed.

Among Bannon's visitors were Kit Tracy and her grandfather, stopping by to leave a loaf of fresh-baked bread wrapped in a towel—a gift from Mary Tracy. It smelled wonderful; he thanked them, a little stiffly, and put the bread on the desk, afterward joining them outside and closing the door so as to shut away the irritating sound of Reub Springer's voice. Orin Tracy scowled and asked, "Does he go on like that all the time?"

"Just about," Bannon said. "He knows he's the center of a storm and I think he enjoys it. I think he really expects the JL to ride in at noon tomorrow and take this jail apart and let him out."

The old man looked seriously troubled. He clawed at his beard, shaking his head as he muttered, "A man gets so he hardly knows what to believe! This here ain't the old Wild West—it's 1904! People just don't go around busting up jails!"

"Luft may not have to try that. There's other kinds of pressure, for a man with his money."

"I just don't understand! I'd never have expected it from John Luft. He's too big a man to act like this—threatening a town!"

Bannon thought wryly, *You admired him too much— you had too many ideas about him and your granddaughter. It ain't easy to wake up to the truth, that he's no better than the tough crew he hires!* Orin Tracy was facing reality, and at his age it had to come hard. Ed Bannon could almost feel sorry for the stiff-necked old man seeing a dream crumble.

He looked at Kit. She was as refreshingly pretty as ever, in the white Sunday dress she'd worn the first day he met her, but she looked as unhappy as her grandfather. It seemed almost that there was a hint of dark stain below her eyes, as though she might have slept badly. He was prompted to say, "I guess you're worried about Bert Maroon. I'm mighty sorry—a fine young man; I can imagine how all his friends must be feeling. Is there any further news from the Weikers?"

She shook her head. "No news." Her voice sounded dull.

A moment later Bannon stood and watched the pair of them start on down the hill, but after a few steps Kit seemed to come to a decision. She said something to her grandfather, sent him on with a pat on the arm; then she was turning back and Bannon wondered what she could want. She stopped before him, putting up a shading hand as she lifted her face to him in the strong sunlight.

"Something I can do?" Bannon asked.

"Oh!" His coolness caused her face to twist, in real pain. Next moment she was blurting out, "I just wanted to tell you—I feel terrible, about day before yesterday! I haven't been able to think about anything except that awful scene we had."

He softened at her obvious sincerity. "I haven't had much luck that way, either," he admitted.

"Some of the things that were said—" Kit shook her head. "I just can't believe myself saying them! I guess you'll have to put it down to jealousy!"

Bannon actually blinked. "Jealousy?"

"Well, what would you expect?" she insisted. "All the time you spent telling me what you did— because you were in love with that Lucy Hardman. It was no way to talk to a girl!"

He could only stare at her. He shook his head. "I've already guessed there's a lot I don't know about dealing with women!" Bannon confessed dryly. "And anyway, *I'm* the one that got jealous— John Luft and that damned motorcar! Though I could tell you didn't really like him too much."

She decided to pass that over. Going back to her opening remark, she repeated: "I'm ashamed of the things I said—accusing you of lying, of trying to put your own blame on the Hardman woman. I should know you well enough, you'd never do a thing like that!"

"I *hope* I wouldn't."

She put out her hand, then, smiling tentatively. "Are we friends again?"

"Far as I'm concerned," he told her earnestly, "we could never be anything less!" At once the sun came out in her face and he took her hand in a warm gesture of reconciliation.

"Grandpa's waiting," she said as she turned to go,

still smiling. "We're on our way down to see Doc Ashby, to find out what he thinks now about poor Bert Maroon. And, of course, to look in on Sam Prentiss."

"Give Sam my regards," Bannon said. "Tell him I may not get in today."

And so, with that cloud lifted, the rest of the day went by in much more bearable fashion for Ed Bannon. Even Springer's grating voice had become little more than a background noise that he failed to respond to, and eventually the big man ran out of talk. After supper Bannon moved a chair outside and tipped it back against the front of the jail, where he sat enjoying the fading light and the sounds of the village—the evening was still enough that he could hear, distinctly, the voices of a church choir singing hymns up on the hill.

He tried not to acknowledge the small but growing tension at work inside him. He believed John Luft to be enough a man of his word that he wouldn't jump the gun on the deadline and make some move under cover of darkness. Nevertheless, as the night deepened, he worked by lamplight in the jail office, cleaning and oiling and checking his six-shooter and a shotgun he found leaning in a corner by the potbellied stove. He didn't really expect gunplay; still, there was no possible way of knowing what the approach of tomorrow's noon might bring.

The real surprise came toward midmorning that Monday of July 11. He returned from checking on his dun and the marshal's animal in the horse shed behind the jail and saw a familiar figure pegging up the steep climb of Nelson Street, moving painfully and leaning on a cane, a gun belt and holster strapped in place about his middle. Bannon muttered an exclamation and hurried to meet him, but Sam Prentiss quickly held up a hand to ward him off. "Let me alone!" the marshal commanded. "I made it this far, I don't need anybody carryin' me the rest of the distance."

"But, Sam!" Bannon protested. "Damn it all, what are you even doing out of bed? Does Doc Ashby know?"

"Ashby? Who's that?" Impatiently, the marshal brushed by him, saying, "Let's not stand out here all morning arguing. I got a hankering to sit down." Bannon could well believe that. He hurried to open the door and Sam Prentiss went stumping inside, leaning heavily on his cane. He eased himself into the desk chair, with a grimace of pain that he wasn't able to disguise. As he laid his cane on top of the desk his hand was trembling.

Looking at the pallor of the marshal's stubbled cheeks, Bannon said accusingly, "I knew it! You sneaked out, didn't you? It's a wonder you ever got up the hill. When Ashby hears about this—"

"Will you quit picking on me?" Sam Prentiss snapped. Looking for the battered, tin alarm clock he added, "What time is it?"

"A little after ten."

"Uh-huh. And with noon coming up, did you really expect me to be anywhere else?"

A looming presence in the dimness of the single jail cell, Reub Springer had been observing all this; now he gave a bark of laughter. "Might as well have stayed in bed, old man! Ain't nobody holding me here, once the JL comes to get me out."

The chair creaked as Sam twisted about in it, a threatening scowl on his face. "You hold your tongue!" he snapped. "I ain't forgetting who I can thank for being in this shape!" At something in his expression or his words, Reub Springer did indeed subside. He stood there clutching the bars, in a sour silence.

Ed Bannon was studying the marshal, trying to judge his condition. "I appreciate you coming," he said now. "And I can understand that you had to. I won't ask how you're feeling—you'd probably lie."

"Then I won't waste my breath. How about some of that coffee I smell brewing?" the old man added. "And is there anything left of the bottle I had in the drawer, there?"

"I haven't touched it . . ."

A couple of shots of the strong, twice-heated coffee, laced from the desk bottle, seemed to do Sam Prentiss some good; his color improved and his voice sounded considerably stronger when he had finished the second cup. He waved aside Bannon's suggestion that he try to make himself comfortable on the cot—he was doing fine, he insisted gruffly, just where he was. He took his gun from its holster, checked the loads, and laid the weapon on the desk within easy reach. After that, the two of them sat talking in desultory tones about nothing very much. In his cell, Reub Springer had fallen to pacing like a caged animal—three steps to the wall and three back again to the barred doorway. Without admitting it, all three were waiting as the hands of the tin clock began to close nearer on twelve.

Mayor Weiker dropped by, fidgety and nervous and with the occasional jumping of a muscle beneath one eye to betray the strain he too was feeling as the deadline neared. He wanted to know if there was anything he could do. Bannon suggested he see about having food sent in, and as he was leaving, Weiker promised he would tend to it. Sure enough, presently a man arrived from the restaurant with a couple of trays. One was passed in to the prisoner. As Bannon and the marshal ate at the desk, they became aware of an occasional shuffling of boots in the street outside, a subdued murmur of voices—some of Mitchell's citizens, it appeared, were gathering, whether merely to watch or perhaps offer a hand in the approaching emergency.

Noon came—and went. The minute hand crept on around the face of the clock. It was half past, and then it was one o'clock. And nothing had happened.

"Your man is late," Ed Bannon commented finally.

Mayor Weiker, who had rejoined them, said with a sudden leap of hope, "I'll bet he changed his mind! He thought it over and realized he'd gone too far and had to back away!"

But Sam Prentiss didn't agree. Waggling his grizzled head the marshal declared, "I don't believe it. More like, he's giving us time to stew. He'll come—when he's ready."

Yet as time continued to drag by and the afternoon stretched out, each passing quarter hour made it less clear what Luft might have in his mind. Perhaps, as Sam suggested, the rancher felt time was in his favor—all he had to do was wait and let his opponents grow fretful as the showdown they had prepared themselves for failed to materialize. Reub Springer, on the other hand, had gone strangely quiet. Springer was no longer boasting, no longer pacing his cell; he sat in there on the bunk, head in hands and staring at the floor. One might have gathered he was having some sober second thoughts.

The crowd outside the jail, grown tired of waiting, soon melted away one by one. The vigil began to take on something of an air of anticlimax. Doc Ashby arrived, hunting his missing patient and very much put out with him. He gave Sam Prentiss a stern lecture for leaving his bed and dressing himself and coming here against orders; but in the face of the marshal's stubbornness there was little he could do about it. To questions about young Maroon he replied curtly that there was nothing new to report and went his way in a bad mood—feeling, like everyone else, the tension they all preferred not to talk about.

It was the man from the restaurant, come to collect his trays and dirty dishes, who said flatly, "Your man ain't going to show. But one thing it looks like to me—we could get us some rain before this day's over."

Bannon stepped outside with him. There had been some clouds, earlier, to make a sporadic dimming and brightening of the light inside the jail. He was surprised now to see how those clouds had increased; they were coming out of the north and west, streaming aloft to the push of air currents that couldn't be felt here on the ground. The restaurant man said, "Well, a little rain wouldn't hurt. The country's been a mite dry lately."

Ed Bannon agreed. Mitchell, with its unfailing flow of springs out of the wall of the canyon, was never apt to lack water enough for its citizens and their gardens. But the rest of this lava-encrusted country needed all it could get, from summer rains and winter blizzards, to maintain a sparse growth of bunchgrass and scrub timber.

Sam Prentiss came stumping out to join them, leaning on his cane as he shared their critical surveyal of the sky. "I dunno," the marshal said darkly. "There could be more rain in that than we know how to handle."

"Oh, come on, now," the restaurant man said, openly amused. "You old-timers—you can't look at a cloud without telling everybody we're in for another waterspout like the one twenty years ago!"

The marshal showed no resentment. "Okay—give it time. One of these days we'll turn out to be right! You don't watch out, you could get your feet damn wet and never even know what happened."

"All right, Sam," the other said with a grin as he started away. "I'll remember. And I'll pass the word along."

"You do that!"

An hour later the day had grown darker still, under a thickening sheet of cloud that turned the sun to a pale, half-seen disk. This time, as he and Bannon stood before the jail, Prentiss pointed with his cane at solid blackness beginning to pile across the southern quarter of the sky. "You see *that*, don't you? Old Bridge Creek, below us here, is fed by a whole slew of creeks that head up in those hills. Let a cloudburst happen and it could funnel a bunch of water down through this canyon, and the creek bed would never hold it. There'd be hell to pay!"

Bannon's thoughts were still busy with John Luft, now hours late for his own deadline. He shrugged and said, "Anything's possible—naturally. But there's no reason to think this would be the day."

A pearly flicker of lightning shuttered through

the gloomy ceiling, and moments later thunder rumbled faintly across the rock-ribbed hills. It occurred to Bannon, who had often watched the uneasy behavior of cattle and horses and wild stock on the range before a storm, that some of the edginess he felt could be due to static electricity building up in the air about him. As the thought crossed his mind, he felt the first touch of a chill wind along the canyon. It breathed against him, and from the direction of the livery stable it brought a sound he recognized—the whicker of a frightened horse.

On an impulse he said, "If it's all right with you, maybe I'll take a look down on Main Street."

"Go ahead," the marshal said, turning back into the jail. "But you're likely to get wet. I think this is going to bust wide open . . ."

Chapter 16

Descending the hill, Bannon already felt the first cold, lancing drops of rain strike his face. From the canyon bottom he could get a better view of the threatening mass of cloud framed at its upper end, where the creek curved from view. All along the street people had come out of the buildings and were nervously watching the storm develop. Now, directly overhead, a brilliant zigzag of lightning suddenly split the sky, followed in seconds by a crash of thunder. Bannon began to hurry as he turned downstream, toward the livery.

As the sky darkened a lantern had been lighted, and it swung in rising wind on a pole before the livery. Its fitful gleam and the shuttering of the lightning showed the horses circling and rearing in the pens and the figures of people scurrying about in purposeful activity. Bannon came upon Kit Tracy, wearing a gleaming slicker and a hat that looked to be an old one of her grandfather's. He caught her arm as she went by, to demand, "What's going on?"

She said breathlessly, "We want to get the horses in. The storm has them scared out of their wits."

"You haven't enough stalls," he pointed out. "Besides, I'm not sure that's what you want to do with them. Supposing the creek was to act up . . ."

The girl had halted to stare at him, while the wind whipped her hair in long strands about her cheeks. "You don't really think it could?"

"Well, Sam Prentiss does—and he was here the other time. It might not hurt to play safe. What do *you* say, Mr. Tracy?" he asked, turning to her grandfather who had come up in time to hear this.

"I say we're in for a helluva storm!" As if to emphasize the old man's words, the whole canyon wavered in a brilliant flare of lightning and was pummeled by a smash of thunder that seemed to break right above their heads. A horse squealed in pure terror. Orin Tracy added, "I've a good mind to try moving these animals!"

"Where to?" asked Bannon.

Tracy waved an arm toward the bench above the canyon. "We can run 'em up Nelson onto the flats and post Howie to keep an eye on them. They'll be high and dry there, and they can't wander far."

"Sounds good. I'll lend a hand."

The black, alone in his pen, seemed to be keeping his head well enough. There was a bridle hanging from a post and Bannon took it with him as he ducked through the poles. The horse whirled away from him, but when Bannon spoke the animal recognized his voice. He stood and let Bannon approach, let him slip the bit into place.

"No handout this time," Bannon said. "We got work to do!" He lifted himself onto the animal's back, without blanket or saddle, and reined over to the gate. The black obeyed the touch of a heel against his flank without any trace of argument.

As Bannon leaned to flip free the loop of wire and

shove the gate open, rain struck him in a solid sheet.
Within seconds, he was soaked to the hide.

Kit had got her little chestnut mare saddled; she
was mounted and her slicker gleamed like metal in
the glow of the wind-tossed lantern, as she struggled
to force the other pen open. Bannon rode to help. It
took work to get the milling and terrified horses
straightened out and headed right. Howie Whipple
came ducking through the barn doorway, mounted
on a rawboned bay—he and Orin Tracy had cleared
the stalls and a dozen horses came ahead of Howie,
into the wild gloaming. Kit and Bannon closed in,
threw all the animals into a bunch and sent them up
the canyon toward Nelson Street, with Orin Tracy
running along behind to wave his arms and help
shout them on.

Rainwater came pouring down the street at them,
in glistening sheets; below, in its bed, the creek tumbled noisily. The figures of men showed, splashing
through the rain, ducking out of the way of the
horses. At the foot of Nelson, Ed Bannon threw himself into turning the animals and pointing them up
the hill in the direction of high ground. And it was
in that moment that he saw Kit Tracy reining toward
him, saw her staring eyes, and saw rather than
heard her mouth form the word *"Listen!"*

He could only nod, dumbly. Above the racket of
the downpour and the clatter of hooves, there was a
new sound such as he had never heard—a swelling
roar, somewhere beyond the blind turn at the
canyon's upper end. Ed Bannon kicked the black
with his heels, at the same time giving a summoning jerk of his arm at Howie Whipple as the latter
shaped up through the murk.

"Get these horses out of here!" he shouted. "Move them, damn it! Here it comes!"

Probably no one in Mitchell was apt to misread that sound. Men who had stood spellbound by the violence of the storm above their heads were suddenly shocked out of inaction. In the canyon itself, there were the startled yells of people beginning a scramble for the nearest point of safety, and along Piety Hill doors were slamming as others, already safe enough, rushed from their houses.

Sam Prentiss heard and levered himself out of his chair as the street outside began to ring to the shouts and running footsteps of people fleeing up the hill. He was at the door when a frantic cry from the cell halted him. Turning he saw Reub Springer clutching the bars, wild-eyed. "Sam! Where you going?"

"Where do you think I'm going? I've waited twenty years to see this, and I don't intend to miss it!" He reached for the knob.

Springer's voice rose to a screech. "No! Goddammit, I'm your prisoner! You can't walk out and leave me to drown like a rat . . ."

The marshal's mouth hardened in contempt. "Take it easy, Reub. You're not going to drown. We're too high up here."

"The hell we are! Open this thing, you hear me? For the love of God, Sam—you got to let me out!" And Springer began to shake the door, with tremendous heavings of muscled arms and shoulders.

Regarding him, seeing the panic in the man's sweating face, Sam Prentiss all at once understood how truly terrified he was. He shrugged impatiently.

"All right—all right, Springer. I'll take you up on the hill. Just try to shut up!"

The marshal hobbled over to the desk for his gun and the key. He had to thrust the cane under his left arm while, to the sound of Springer's tortured breathing, he fitted the key into the lock. The rush of the approaching flood seemed almost enough now to shake the building.

The key turned, and as it did, a sudden thrust by the man in the cell sent the barred door slamming open, full into the marshal. He was thrown off balance and before he could bring up the revolver Reub Springer was on him. A blow from a muscled forearm drove Sam Prentiss into the wall; a fist struck his jaw. His knees buckled and he fell forward, Springer letting him go limply down upon his face.

Breathing heavily, Reub Springer stood a moment looking at the motionless shape of the lawman. He saw the six-shooter the marshal had dropped and he leaned and picked it up. At the same moment he became aware again of the voices outside and the swelling roar in the upper canyon. That roused him. He turned quickly, his boot striking the cane and sending it clattering. In a couple of strides he reached the door of the jail, cracked it open. The people in the street seemed concerned only with getting away from the danger below them. Reub Springer was sure no one noticed him as he eased through the opening and, quickly, out of sight around the corner of the building.

At almost that instant the flood hit Mitchell.

A thirty-foot wall of water—turgid, dirty yellow in the fading light—swept around the upper curve of the canyon carrying a freight of house-sized boulders and entire uprooted trees. With incredible ferocity it fell upon the lower town. The first house was lifted and tossed into the air like a cracker box and carried on, riding the crest. A larger building— it was Wilcey Chipman's saloon—slewed about on its foundation and then crumbled as though swatted by a powerful hand. And after that, each structure that made up Tiger Town received in turn the smashing impact of those tons of runoff. Buildings were tumbled and flung against one another and disintegrated, and the tide swept on.

It seemed to happen in slow motion, yet it could have taken only minutes. The high crest moved on down the canyon and almost at once the creek began to subside again within its banks. But where Main Street had been, now only muddy waters swirled and eddied, with scarcely anything to indicate this was once the heart of a town. Above, gathered along the rim of the canyon, the people of Mitchell stood drenched and shocked to silence, pummeled by the heavy downpour and with the wild display of thunder and lightning breaking endlessly about them.

Wind knifing through rain-soaked clothing, Ed Bannon lifted his head finally, to peer about at the stunned and silent faces. He heard a child crying. There was no way to tell yet whether everyone had managed to get clear or if some might have been caught in that wild rush of water. If so, the chances were slim that they would have survived it. Those he saw had their lives, at least, and the homes up here on the bench were safe. But there were many who would have lost everything.

He saw Wilcey Chipman, his face a sick and haggard mask; the fancy cherry-wood bar and all the expensive fixings of Chipman's saloon were gone now. Bannon thought of Doc Ashby, and the garden and fruit trees of which he'd been so proud, to say nothing of his medical books and supplies and the surgical equipment. And what of Jess Weiker's Emporium, with its well-stocked shelves? Nothing left there, of course. Could a man survive, in wealth or in spirit, a ruinous blow like that?

He shook his head at these thoughts. And then, as the stricken people on the canyon rim began to stir from the grip of first shock, he turned and there was Kit Tracy. Her rain-wet features were distraught as she clutched at his arm and cried, above the continuing noise of the storm, "Ed! Have you seen Grandpa?"

Something turned over inside him. "Why—no, Kit. Not since we moved out with the horses. He was on foot, helping get them started."

"The last thing I remember was him saying he'd forgotten to fetch the cashbox from the office . . . Do you suppose—?"

Bannon had caught sight of Mary Tracy, wrapped in an old sweater and with a shawl over her head. He turned the girl gently, saying briefly, "Stay with your grandmother, Kit. You'd better try to get her inside. I'll see what I can find out."

He was cold with the certainty that it was hopeless, but at such a moment any kind of activity had to be a welcome relief. He had left the black stud with Howie Whipple; on foot he dropped down the hill into Nelson Street, taking the steep slant toward what had once been Main. It was easy enough to make out the high mark of the flood—it had even reached part way up Nelson, though not as far as the jail building.

Suddenly he was ankle-deep in silt and swirling water that sucked at his boots, slickly treacherous.

Fighting it, Bannon turned downstreet and now he saw that, by some freak of the flood, the big livery barn was still standing. It had been grievously pummeled, of course, twisted off its base and smashed against the side of the canyon; all its timbers were sprung, much of its roof fallen in. A touch seemed enough to knock it down.

Bannon waded toward it through the muck and the litter of boulders and broken trees the water had spilled through the canyon, the raw, rank smell of the flood in his nostrils. In the yawning and misshapen doorway of the barn he paused to call Orin Tracy's name; only the drum of unceasing rain and a mutter of thunder from the retreating storm answered him. There was little light to see by. He went inside the building, prepared at any moment to have the broken roof timbers give way and collapse on him.

The office door had been sprung out of its frame. He had to force it open and saw what was left of desk and chairs, strewn and splintered, and a floating litter of sodden books and papers. He turned away, supposing he would have to look into each separate stall just on the chance that the old man's body might have lodged in one of them, instead of being swept on down with the current.

A voice said, "Bannon!"

He froze. Then, in turning toward the wide doorway, he moved so quickly that he nearly lost his footing in the slick mud and swirling water. His eyes refused at first to believe what he saw. Bulking against the gray light outside, Reub Springer stood on boots planted wide apart; and the gun in his big hand was a potent threat.

Bannon looked at the gun. He found the voice to

put the question that came first to his mind: "How the devil did you get loose? Where's Sam Prentiss? Have you done anything to him?"

"Oh, I done something to him," Reub Springer said. "I dunno how bad—I didn't stop to find out. *You're* the one I'm interested in." He lifted his other hand; he curled it into a fist and crooked the forefinger, a summoning gesture. "You come over here, boy, so I can get a better look at you." When Bannon stood unmoving, the big man's head lifted and he became peremptory. "I said, walk! I want you out here. I want to be able to see the look on your face."

There was no choice. Bannon's own gun and belt were where he had left them, hanging on their peg at the jail, when he came hurrying down the hill to offer his help with moving the stable horses. Where he stood, there was no way to move, no place to go that he might hope to reach before a bullet from the ready six-shooter could strike him down. Slowly, setting his boots carefully, he waded toward the frame-sprung doorway and Springer drew back to give him room. He came out of the shadow of the broken roof, and the thinning spears of rain stung his face as he halted and stood waiting for what the other man would do next.

Springer said heavily, "You been asking for this—and what you done to me night before last cinched it!" His face looked oddly lopsided with the swelling from the blow of Ed Bannon's gun barrel. He lifted a hand and touched the place and nodded. "You poleax a man, you ought to do it hard enough to keep!"

Bannon said coldly, "So you're going to shoot me. And then what? I don't see any horse. How far will you get without one?"

"Let *me* worry about that!" the big man retorted. "You won't be worrying about nothing. Because you—"

They must both have heard in the same instant. Bannon's reaction was one of disbelief. Yet having once known that sound, he could never again mistake it. He heard himself exclaiming, "Springer! For God's sake—*there's going to be another one!*"

Springer had half turned his head to stare up the canyon toward the swelling rumble that warned of what was coming. Now he turned back and Bannon knew, from the look of his face, not even a second flood would keep him from the purpose that was locked in his mind. And knowing this, Ed Bannon moved.

Silt and water clutched at his ankles as he made his lunge. The gun in Springer's hand went off, the flat report all but lost in the growing tumult of rushing water. At the last moment Bannon had been able to strike the big man's wrist, knock it high, and throw the shot wide. He grabbed and caught at the sleeve, and after that they were struggling in mud and swirling water, Springer trying to tear free and Bannon fighting for a grip on the hand that held the gun. They slipped and both went down, and for an instant Bannon's face was buried in muck. He lost his hold on Springer, rolled to his knees, snorting to clear his head. A couple of yards distant Reub Springer was floundering and threshing about, trying to find purchase and get his feet under him. And Bannon saw the man had lost his gun.

He appeared to think that a small matter. He looked about, seeking his enemy, and, finding him, came for him to do the job with his bare hands. Ed Bannon tried to evade their reach, shouting,

"Springer! Use your head, for God's sake!" But if Reub Springer was even aware of the torrent that had come racing into sight now, around the upward bend of the canyon, he seemed indifferent to it in his single-minded need to lay hands on his enemy.

This second wall of water bearing down on them was less precipitous than the first had been, but it came on with a speed that vanquished thought and short-circuited reflexes. Seeking a way to escape it, Bannon could not cope with Springer's mindless attack. He tried to back away, slipped again, and went to one knee, and before he could rise again the other man had him. They went down together, rolling, and big hands found Bannon's throat and closed on it. He struck out, blinded by silt, felt his fist strike the other man's head and bounce off futilely. The hands at his throat clamped harder; his chest began to burn and the roaring of his own pulse filled his ears.

Then a stronger force than either of them lifted them up and spun them and tore them apart. Tossing in the churning flood, Bannon had a confused impression of cloud-filled sky and muddy water and canyon walls, blurred and dizzying. He saw what was left of Orin Tracy's livery collapse into jackstraws and sweep away on the eddying current. He had a glimpse—no more—of Reub Springer's head spinning like a cork and abruptly vanishing as a broken section of what looked to be nearly half a tree trunk bore down upon him.

In the next breath Bannon found himself whirled high and flung solidly into the branches of a tree growing out of the side of the canyon. He crashed into it, felt limb ends stab him with what felt like a hundred blunt spearpoints. He didn't feel anything else . . .

Chapter 17

He grew aware of sunlight stabbing into his eyes. He blinked and tried to duck his head away from it and realized then that he was staring directly into a rift in the clouds, somewhere over in the direction of Bailey Butte, with the rays of the lowering sun turning a few diminishing streaks of rain into slashes of gold. After that a shadow moved between him and the sun; he was lying on wet and soggy ground, with a knot of men surrounding him.

When he made a move to push himself up, one of these said, "Hey—go easy! The knocking around you took in that water, no telling but you could be pretty badly bunged up." And someone else told him, "It took three of us to put a rope on you and haul you out of that tree you piled up in."

Bannon thanked them for it. He didn't remember very much. He knew he had taken a battering, and aching muscles protested when he tried to move; he didn't think he had taken any worse damage than that. He shook his head impatiently when they tried to keep him where he was. He said, "I'm all right," and got a little unsteadily to his feet. Urgencies crowded in on him. He demanded, "What about Reub Springer?"

"Is *that* who you were fighting with?" the first man exclaimed. "When the waterspout come through?

Somebody said it was, but—hell, I understood you had him in jail! Anyway, he's gone now, Bannon— we all saw it. A snag hit him and he went under and never showed again."

"Small loss!" a third man commented sourly. "From where I stood, it looked like he was trying to kill you."

"He had it in mind," Ed Bannon agreed.

They were standing at the very edge of the drop-off, where they'd pulled him up; the rope they used lay coiled nearby. He took a step closer for a look. Only minutes could have passed; the creek had only just begun subsiding after the second head of water roared through. Anything left of Main Street earlier had been scoured clean this time. Of the wreckage of the big livery barn, not a trace remained.

A man said, "We all figure what must have happened, those clouds burst over Bridge Creek and then crossed the divide to Keyes Creek and dumped a second load—that could explain it coming down on us in two bunches. A good thing! If it had hit us all at once, no saying what the damage would have been . . ."

Ed Bannon thanked them again and moved away, feeling a need to do something more than stand here talking.

Overhead the storm seemed ended as quickly as it began; the whole mass of clouds was breaking in a marbling pattern of dazzle. The wind that blew along the bench cut through his soaked clothing clear to the flesh, which felt as though it must be a mass of bruises—that tree might have saved his life, but it had punished him too. Suddenly he heard his name and here was Kit Tracy, hurrying toward him, her face holding a look of disbelief.

She came straight into his arms, her own arms going tight about him; he winced a little from the pain of bruised ribs. Kit's cheek pressed against his soaked shirt and he heard her saying, between the sobs he could feel wracking her, "Oh, Ed! I can't believe it! When you went off down the hill and that second wave struck—I was sure I'd never see you again!"

"It's all right," he said, patting her shoulder awkwardly. "It's really all right . . ." And then he looked up and saw Orin Tracy watching them. Bannon stared, above the crown of the old hat on the girl's head, seeing now the metal cashbox tucked under her grandfather's elbow. "Where did you come from?"

The old man looked as astonished as Bannon felt. "I could ask you the same thing! We sure enough figured you a goner. How in the world did you manage?"

"I still don't know for certain," Bannon told him. "I'd have to call it luck."

"It'd been my fault if you were killed," Orin Tracy admitted. He seemed not to be aware, or at least not to mind, that this man had his granddaughter in his arms. "I'd saved my money and got out in plenty of time. I just never stopped to think that the girl would be worried or that she'd send you to look for me. And of course, none of us could know there was a second waterspout on the way!"

"Well, it missed its chance at me," Bannon said, trying to pass the matter off. "Was there anyone you know of who didn't turn out that lucky?"

Since they seemed not to have heard about Reub Springer's death, he decided he would rather say nothing of that just yet.

Kit disengaged herself to answer his question, troubled at what she had to report. "So far we've only heard of one person that died. That was poor Martin Smith—he was ninety years old, and he'd gone to bed early. They got his wife out in time, but before his daughter could go back for him it was too late. She told me all she was able to do was stand and watch the creek carry the house away and smash it to kindling!" She pushed the damp hair back from her face. "We can only hope there won't turn out to be more."

Her grandfather added, "It remains to be seen what damage was done, on down the creek. The telephone went out, of course, first thing. But I hear one of the boys had presence of mind to jump on a horse and race off ahead of the flood. He just may have been able to spread the word in time to save some lives downstream, between here and the John Day."

Bannon would have made some comment, but now the girl exclaimed, "You must be freezing! You're soaked through. You've got to change into something dry before you catch your death."

"I have some other clothes at the jail," he said. "I was just now heading for there."

"You do that," Orin Tracy told him. "Katherine and I had best get back to helping whatever of these people we can . . ." He took his granddaughter's arm, but as they started away the old man hesitated and turned back. "First," he said gruffly, like a man not easily given to voicing thanks, "I must say I'm deeply obliged to you—helping us save our stock and then going back down there to look for me when Katherine was worried."

"No need to mention it."

But the old man shook his head, pawing at his beard in a way he had when he faced an uncomfortable situation. "I'm afraid I've said some things I wish now I hadn't," he insisted. "I wish you'd consider 'em unsaid."

"I can't think what they could have been," Ed Bannon lied, and he stood a moment to watch the pair of them as they moved away.

Late sunlight lay golden, now, all along Piety Hill, striking a glint from every wet surface left by the storm. Around him, people who had been stunned by the disaster to their town were still moving about, almost silently, in a daze of incomprehension. As had happened once before, the inhabitants of Mitchell would have to set about picking up the pieces and reassembling the wreckage into a living community.

Somehow Ed Bannon didn't doubt that they would; this was home to them. Moreover, as more than one person had pointed out to him, the canyon with its never-failing springs was an oasis in a country that offered few places where they could grow their lush gardens and live so well, with so little effort. They weren't the sort to give it all up, even after this kind of setback . . .

Turning in at the jail, Bannon saw Doc Ashby coming down the hill and nodded to him but did not pause—he was thinking of Sam Prentiss, remembering Reub Springer's dark hint of having done something to the marshal. When he saw the open door to the cell and the motionless shape sprawled on the floor in front of it, he quickly turned back and gave the doctor an urgent, summoning gesture. Ashby broke at once into a run; Bannon entered the jail and was kneeling by the unconscious lawman when the doctor came in. Ashby closed the street door and moved to join him.

Sam Prentiss was breathing, shallowly but regularly; his color looked all right, but the left side of his jaw was bruised and swollen. Bannon hadn't touched him, leaving that for the expert hands of the doctor. He watched anxiously while Ashby felt for a pulse, used thumb and forefinger to pry open an eyelid. That had an effect. Prentiss moaned a little, in protest, and twisted his head aside. He opened his eyes then and rolled them about, looking fuddled and disoriented. He muttered something incoherent.

Ashby told him, "You're all right, Sam. Somebody gave you a real wallop. But you're coming around."

Remembering the bottle in the desk, Bannon went to fetch it and a cup. The doctor poured a little of the whiskey and then, lifting the lawman's shoulders, got a couple of swallows into him. Prentiss coughed a time or two, eyes watering, but after that his head seemed clearer. Ashby set the cup aside and told Bannon, "Help me get him up on the cot—he'll be more comfortable."

They lifted him and propped him there with his shoulders against the wall. Ashby said, "Now, Sam. Can you tell us what happened?"

The whiskey had loosened the marshal's tongue, brought him the rest of the way to consciousness. "That Springer!" he grunted. "He's got a fist would floor a mule! My damn jaw feels like it's sprung . . ." He put up a hand uncertainly and winced as he felt of the swelling.

"But how did he get out of that cell?" Bannon wanted to know.

"Like a fool, I let him!" Sam Prentiss said. "It happened when we heard—" With returning memory his eyes widened in horror; he clutched at Bannon's arm. "Oh, my God!" he cried. "I wasn't dreaming that, was I? We *did* hear it?"

Ashby nodded. "Yes, Sam. You heard. There's been a flood—a hell of a flood!"

Prentiss would have surged up off the bunk then, but Ed Bannon held him back; the man was still weak enough that it required no great effort. "Easy!" he warned. "Wait till you get your strength back. I'm afraid you missed that one. There's not a lot left of the town, but what there is will wait for you. All right?" Sam Prentiss nodded, and he took the restraining hand away. "You were telling us about Reub Springer . . ."

The marshal made a face. "I should of knowed better. But, hell! He completely panicked. I tried to tell him he was safe, but he thought sure he'd drown in that cell. He wasn't pretending, either—I could tell he was scared to death, completely out of his head. So I said all right, I'd take him up on the hill. Only, the minute I got the door unlocked—he done this to me!" He touched his jaw, gingerly. "I don't suppose he lost any time, getting the hell out of town!"

"As a matter of fact—" Ed Bannon started to say, but he got no further. For that was when the street door was suddenly flung open, and Mayor Weiker put his head through. His color was bad, his eyes distracted. He gave his message without focusing on who was in the room.

"It's the JL!" he announced. "They're here . . ."

Bannon swore. In the events of the past hour he had lost all thought of John Luft and his threats and his deadline, which had long since come and past.

Quickly on his feet, he had reached the door before remembering he was unarmed. He went back for his gun, grabbing belt and holster from their peg and slinging them in place about his hips as he hurried outside. In the slanted light of the low-hanging sun he took the few steep yards to the foot of Nelson and halted there as he saw them.

There were a score or more in the cavalcade. They had come up the canyon road, putting their horses over the crossing that still ran deep and swift in the wake of the flood. Now they rode at a walk over fetlock-deep mud where the lower town had stood, through the litter of boulders and uprooted trees, the remains of building foundations, even some scattered pieces of heavy machinery lying about, half buried. Bannon saw disbelief on some of their faces as they stared about them.

John Luft, in the van of his crew as usual, seemed to have added a few additional recruits; perhaps he thought he needed them. Bannon's eyes narrowed as he picked out Nick Garvey and Garvey's friends Jeff Pitts and Harry Ruser—so, Reub Springer's special cronies had been given roles in this. And riding in Springer's old place, alongside Luft's stirrup, was someone he had never expected to see.

At sight of Frank Conger, Bannon stiffened. Still, it made sense. The man hunter would not have been wasting time since their abortive confrontation in the restaurant. He must have looked into the state of affairs in the Mitchell country, had seen how things stood, and elected to throw in his lot with someone with power whose interests here seemed to match his own.

Needless to say he had found himself another

gun; it was strapped on a cartridge belt around his middle.

Knowing now what he faced, Ed Bannon set his shoulders and waited as Luft brought his riders to a halt. All this time a crowd had been gathering, streaming down off the hill. A quick glance about him showed Bannon the bleak expressions of men who had just lost their town, but who were now ready to meet this new danger with a challenge in their faces and with weapons of various kinds—pistols and hunting rifles and at least one double-barreled shotgun.

Sam Prentiss was there as well, leaning on his cane, together with Doc Ashby who must have known there was no way to keep the wounded marshal out of this. Among the others, Bannon saw the mayor and even, toward the back, Kit Tracy and her grandfather. He shook his head at them, trying to warn them almost anything could happen, that this was no place for them to be. But so far, the townspeople were merely waiting, and now John Luft, having pulled in, threw a long look over the desolation about him and said, without preliminary, "You people have got yourselves a mess!"

"Did you come to gloat?" Ed Bannon suggested.

"Why, we didn't even know," the rancher told him. "Not until just now, riding up the canyon—that's the first hint we had that there must have been considerable of a washout. Not much left, is there?"

Jess Weiker moved up beside Bannon. "It cleaned out the whole lower town!" he said heavily. "Twenty-eight buildings, by my count. That's the machinery from the flour mill that you see, scattered along the bottom."

Luft gave it all another long survey. "I suppose the lot of you will be moving out, now."

"Moving out?" the mayor exclaimed. "What are you talking about? This is our town—our home. We're just going to have to rebuild."

"So that, in another twenty years maybe, it can all happen again? Now, that really makes a lot of sense!"

At the sarcasm in the rancher's voice, Ed Bannon felt his temper beginning to slip. "Wouldn't you say it's for them to decide?"

"The way we look at it," Mayor Weiker pointed out, "there'll always be need of a town hereabouts, and we don't know any other spot for it as likely as this particular canyon. We at least have a place up here on the bench, that's safe for our families to live. That being so, we figure we can take the risk of maybe having to rebuild a few business houses. Folks who live in Mitchell are kind of stubborn."

"Yes, I've noticed that," the rancher said dryly. His voice hardened, then, as he got down to the matter at hand. "I'm some stubborn, myself. Right now I'm going to ask you just one question and I want a straight answer: what about the Maroon kid?"

"Bert? Oh, he's doing a lot better," Weiker said. "He came out of the coma awhile ago—hungry enough to eat a horse."

Luft sought out Ashby. "How about it, Doc? Do you confirm this?"

The doctor nodded. "The boy suffered a concussion, but it looks as though he'll be all right. Most likely what he needs now is quiet and good care—and he's been getting the best, from Jess Weiker's missus and their girl."

"Glad to hear it—because, with him in the clear, it

means you've no further excuse to be holding my range boss in that jail. I've been more than patient up to now; I've given you plenty of chance to think matters over. But this time I won't leave without him!"

There was a moment that seemed to hold its breath. A horse, feeling its rider's tension, stomped and moved around a little and had to be brought back to control. Bannon was the one gave Luft his answer: "We're agreed. Mitchell has got enough other problems, now. I think everybody would be more than satisfied to have you take him out of this town and see that he stayed out. Only, we can't do it. Reub Springer is dead. The flood caught him and carried him off."

The news didn't seem to register at first; then it was as though a shock wave hit the men from the JL. Only Frank Conger, looking on, failed to show any reaction at all. Someone among Springer's friends began to curse, and Luft himself lifted his head to stare blankly at Ed Bannon. He exclaimed, "Let me hear you say that again! And you'd better be joking!"

It was Sam Prentiss who told him, "Nobody jokes about a thing like that! I let your man out of the cell because he was scared witless and sure the flood would get him. Turned out he should have stayed where he was."

"You're lying!" Nick Garvey shouted from the pack of horsemen. "You're all lying! Hell, Reub was too smart for that. If he's dead, the town murdered him!"

"You couldn't be more wrong," Ed Bannon retorted. "*Springer* was the one who tried to make it murder! He came after me and caught me without a gun. But then the water hit us, and I'm just lucky I got out alive."

"I hope you're listening," Jess Weiker told Luft then. "Because everything he's saying is the truth! A lot of us saw what happened. If you force us to, we're prepared to back him up!"

But Ed Bannon threw up a hand, raising his voice to make himself heard before matters could get out of control. "No! The rest of you stay out of it, Weiker. This is between me and Luft—and it has been, from the day I hit this place. So if you've got to blame somebody for killing your range boss," he told the cowman, "lay it on me."

John Luft studied him. "On you . . ." he echoed, in a dangerous tone. "You're really sure this is how you want it?"

"I'm sure!" Bannon was experiencing a swell of reckless anger that had been too long bottled up and threatened now to spill over. "I know your kind, Luft, and I've just about had a bellyful! I let one of you drive me out of Montana, rather than stand up to him. But that once was enough. This time I'm standing my ground!

"Men like you seem to think because you have money it puts you above the law and even above common courtesy. You think you can do anything at all that suits you—run a man into the ground or boycott a town out of existence. Well, some day, somebody's going to bring it home to you that you're not that special!"

Luft had heard him out, scowling furiously. He seemed more astonished than anything else at being spoken to in this way. He drew himself straight in the saddle. He said harshly, "You got a rough tongue, mister!"

"But he's telling you something you been needing to hear!" Marshal Prentiss retorted. "You're raising a powerful fuss over nothing. Hell! Nobody murdered Springer—he got himself killed, and I think you know it. In any case, he wasn't worth making a war over. Which is just what you'll get from this town, if you go after Ed Bannon!"

Luft glared at the marshal. In a dangerous stillness he looked at all these men who faced him here in the last glow of sunlight, surrounded by the ravages of the flood that had destroyed Mitchell. From the angry stiffness of his face, Bannon judged that some very heavy thoughts were at work behind it; the rancher's eyes appeared to be almost unseeing.

"Well?" Sam Prentiss challenged.

Abruptly, with no change of expression, John Luft gave a pull at the reins that turned his horse in the slick mud underfoot. To his men he said gruffly, "Oh, hell! Let's go!"

Nobody moved; they simply failed to understand. Finding himself met by silence, the rancher lifted his head and the impatient stare he laid about him contained all the man's arrogant authority. "Let's go, I said! Can't you see, these people have got a town to build . . ."

It must have come through, then, that he actually meant it. An exchange of baffled looks passed among the horsemen, but after that reins were hauled in, saddle leather creaked as horses began to make their turns in the crowded space of Nelson Street. Only a few of the men refused to yield, holding firm and making the rest move around them; these, however, weren't members of the JL crew. Frank Conger for one stayed just where he was, and his eyes were fixed, not on John Luft, but on Bannon. The latter met his look, certain at last that the moment had come.

Without warning a rider came pushing forward, boots flailing the sides of his mount as a cry of rage burst from him. It was Nick Garvey. Bannon saw the gun lifting and grabbed at his own holster, but too late. A shot sounded. Bannon took a blow on the upper arm that knocked him spinning. He struck the ground hard, the gun's report mingling in his head with startled shouts and the squeal of horses and one piercing scream that he somehow knew must have come from Kit Tracy.

Dazed, but with reflexes set toward self-protection, he lay on the rain-soaked ground and groped for his revolver, only to realize that it must have fallen out of the holster. Looking up he saw Nick Garvey, through a film of powder smoke, and without quite comprehending, he saw the metal of a gun reflecting sunlight as Frank Conger lifted his arm and brought it down, hard. The battered hat flew from Garvey's skull. The gun dropped out of his hand and he doubled forward and went down out of saddle, to land limply on the ground among the horses.

The man hunter instantly leveled his revolver on Jeff Pitts and Harry Ruser, catching Garvey's friends before either one could move. "Don't try anything!" Conger said harshly. "Don't even think about it . . ."

Everything stopped. John Luft, already riding away, had halted and turned back as he heard the shot, but he too seemed confused and unable to do more than stare. It was Sam Prentiss who stepped forward and lifted his cane, to point it at Pitts and at Ruser, in turn. His expression was terrible as he cried, "You—and you! The two of you put that man across his saddle and get him out of here. Snap to it!"

They flicked a look at Conger for permission. Then, terrified, the pair of them scrambled off their horses and laid hold of their friend, who stirred and moaned faintly. Nick Garvey came up off the ground, completely limp in their hands, and grunting with the effort they threw him facedown on his own saddle. After they had hurriedly remounted, Sam Prentiss gave them final warning, "I don't want to see any of you in this town ever again. You hear?"

They heard. Ruser grabbed the reins of Garvey's horse and they were leaving that place fast, the unconscious man bouncing and swaying. The cavalcade from JL split apart to make way for them, and in minutes they were gone.

During this, Kit Tracy had pushed through and dropped on her knees beside Ed Bannon, and now Doc Ashby was there as well, saying, "Let me see that arm!" Bannon waved him away. He saw Frank Conger edging his horse over toward him, gun still in hand. Bannon made another hopeless try for his own lost weapon—and then, unexpectedly, felt the revolver's handle being slipped into his fingers. He glanced aside, to look into Kit's face streaming with tears. Gratefully he tightened his grip on the gun's handle, weak as he was and drained of strength by the shock of the bullet he'd taken. Lying on his back in the mud, he tried to lift the heavy six-shooter as the man hunter loomed above him.

For a long moment they looked at each other. And Conger slid his gun into its holster and asked, irrelevantly, "Can someone tell me, where's the nearest telegraph?"

Bannon could only stare at him, confused, unable to make any sense of the question. It was Kit who, in a trembling voice, managed an answer: "Fossil. It's the county seat . . ."

Frank Conger nodded. "Thanks. I find I have to send a wire," he went on to explain, his voice flat and without expression. "I have to report to someone that I've failed the job he hired me for. Looks like the man I was after has taken off for California—it's hardly worth trying to locate a trail, now. But, a man can't always expect to win!"

Of those who heard him, it would have been a complete mystery to any except for Kit and, probably, Sam Prentiss. It brought Ed Bannon struggling to his feet, managing shakily with the girl's help. Fighting the throb of bullet-scored muscles in his shoulder, he looked up at the man hunter and said gruffly, "I don't understand you!"

"Don't try." Conger kneed the gray closer, and this time when he spoke it was for Kit and Bannon, alone. "The way you stood up to us, a minute ago—well, let's just say I feel a little ashamed, sometimes, of the business I'm in!" He didn't wait for an answer, but abruptly pulled rein and spun his horse and went off across the flat in the direction of the creek crossing.

He was the last to leave; yonder, Luft and the JL crew were already splashing over. And the crowd in Nelson Street broke up as the men of Mitchell, their moment of crisis ended, went streaming off to find a vantage point and watch the cavalcade depart.

Doc Ashby and the marshal passed Kit and Bannon, on their way back to the jail; Ashby touched Bannon on the shoulder and said sternly, "You come along. I want to tend to that arm!"

The other man nodded without looking at him. He stood motionless amidst all this activity, too stunned as yet to move. Kit, beside him, found the voice to ask, "Did he really mean it? He's going to pull that man Hardman off?"

"Conger wouldn't have said a thing he didn't mean."

She exclaimed, "But you see what it does—you're *free!* You can forget all of that, because you're free now to go anywhere, do anything you like . . ."

Ed Bannon looked at her, and then he looked at the devastation on the flat below them, softening with the settling of dusk. He said slowly, "I don't know. Right now, I'm not sure I'm in a hurry to go anywhere. There's your grandfather's livery stable—there's a whole town needs to be rebuilt. And, if anyone knows a way a man with a sore arm can help, wouldn't be too hard convincing me I want a part in the building."

He knew by her look that it was the answer she'd been hoping, and even praying, she might hear.

D(wight) B(ennett) Newton is the author of a number of notable Western novels. Born in Kansas City, Missouri, Newton went on to complete work for a Master's degree in history at the University of Missouri. From the time he first discovered Max Brand in Street and Smith's *Western Story Magazine*, he knew he wanted to be an author of Western fiction. He began contributing Western stories and novelettes to the Red Circle group of Western pulp magazines published by Newsstand in the late 1930s. During the Second World War, Newton served in the US Army Engineers and fell in love with the central Oregon region when stationed there. He would later become a permanent resident of that state and Oregon frequently serves as the locale for many of his finest novels. As a client of the August Lenniger Literary Agency, Newton found that every time he switched publishers he was given a different byline by his agent. This complicated his visibility. Yet in notable novels from *Range Boss* (1949), the first original novel ever published in a modern paperback edition, through his impressive list of titles for the Double D series from Doubleday, *The Oregon Rifles, Crooked River Canyon,* and *Disaster Creek* among them, he produced a very special kind of Western story. What makes it so special is the combination of characters who seem real and about whom a reader comes to care a great deal and Newton's fundamental humanity, his realization early on (perhaps because of his study of history) that little that happened in the West was ever simple but rather made desperately complicated through the conjunction of numerous opposed forces working at cross purposes. Yet, through all of the turmoil on the frontier, a basic human decency did emerge. It was this which made the American frontier experience so profoundly unique and which produced many of the remarkable human beings to be found in the world of Newton's Western fiction.